When It

Happens

To You

SISTERHOOD CHRONICLES 4

ANITA DAVIS

ISBN-10: 1-946721-06-9
ISBN-13: 978-1-946721-06-8

Books may be purchased in quantity by contacting the author
Anita Davis
Set Apart Publishing
PO Box 39229
Chicago, IL 60659-0229
or by email at authoranitadavis@gmail.com

ACKNOWLEDGEMENTS

I want to thank God and my couch for helping me write this book.

Thank you to anyone else who helped but I may not have mentioned by name.

This is dedicated to and in memory of my Aunt Doretha, Auntie Yvonne, and Cousin Minnie who lived rich lives but lost their battles with cancer. I thank God for having each of you in my life in the way I did.

ENJOY

Death is not the greatest loss in life.
The greatest loss is what dies inside us
while we live.

Norman Cousins

1

"I can't believe you had the nerve to run off and elope," Kim said as she coughed into a napkin with one hand and popped one of her dearest friends, Pam, on the arm with her other hand.

"Ouch." Pam rubbed her arm as she looked over her shoulder at Kim.

"You either." Kim popped Vance as she walked past him headed towards her seat at the end of the table.

"Hey, it wasn't my doing. I kept asking her if she was sure she wanted to do it that way and not have you all there, but she insisted we elope. And who was I to deny my beautiful bride her desire." Smiling, Vance turned to stare at Pam who was already cheesing and staring at him. They both puckered their lips as the magnetic love between them drew them closer until they shared a passionate kiss. It was abruptly interrupted by the balled-up napkin that hit both of them in the face.

Kim was the offender.

Pam stuck her neck out to see past Vance and stared Kim down. Her beady eyes focused on Kim as her forehead crinkled and her nostrils flared.

Everyone else stared silently at Pam as she pressed her lips tightly together.

Kim tilted her head to the side and stared back at Pam. Her mouth curved lopsided and a brow lifted. Her face read as if to say, "Yeah, I threw it. Whatchu gonna do?"

Everyone in the kitchen broke out in laughter.

Pam threw the balled-up napkin back at Kim. "I know you're upset you weren't there, but don't throw things at me and my husband." Pam winked at Kim as she giggled and closed in on Vance to steal another quick kiss from him.

Everyone could see Kim revving up to combat Pam with one of her signature in-your-face comebacks, but when she opened her mouth, out came another cough.

"Are you okay?" Monica's brows furrowed as she looked at Kim.

Darius was at her side soon with a glass of water. "Here, drink some."

Kim looked up at him with a raised eyebrow, but her need to cough stifled any response she may have given him. He was being too affectionate towards her as far as she was concerned, but she took the glass from his outstretched arm anyway.

They weren't a couple, merely cuddle buddies, even though they didn't cuddle when they were together. Darius was one of Vance's closest friends and attended a barbecue Vance was hosting as principal of the elementary school to show his gratitude for his staff's hard work throughout the school year. Darius stood in one section of the parking lot joking with the fellas but never taking his eyes off Kim, while she sat with her best friend and colleague Pam oogling Darius every chance she got. When the two finally locked eyes, they knew their powerful attraction to one another would spell greatness in bed. It did and ever since then, they worked tirelessly, round after round, to satisfy one another between the sheets.

Kim was hoping the lingering stares he graced her with all night didn't mean that he wanted more from her than what she was willing to give him. He was her latest, but couldn't be her last. She wouldn't go back on the promise she made to herself in undergrad. She needed her recent bout of coughing to end soon, before the sisterhood questioned her more than their wary stares did so.

She took a sip of water, cleared her throat, and spoke up putting that hint of sass in her voice everyone in the room had become familiar with. "Don't look at me like that, Missy." She stared directly at Monica. "I'm fine. My food just went down the wrong pipe." She hit her chest with a closed fist demonstrating that she would soon be fine once the food lodged in her pipes dissipated.

"Food? What food?" Renee, Kim's triplet sister, said pointing to her plate. "This spread Monica laid out to celebrate Pam and Vance's nuptials is food. But you call that, as you would say, 'bird food' on your plate food?" Renee waved her arm over platters full of fried chicken, cornbread, spaghetti, macaroni, collard greens, corn, dressing, apple pie, and quite a few others desserts one would see gracing a table for thanksgiving dinner, even though it was nowhere near thanksgiving.

"Mind your business." Kim snarled at Renee. "I'm watching my figure."

"Darius has that task under control," Vance chimed in and soon pounded Darius' fist.

Darius winked at Kim and then made his way back to where he once stood leaning against the dual-level granite top island in Monica and Keith's open kitchen-dining area.

"You're slimming down awfully quick," Renee said with a raised eyebrow. "I hope you really aren't trying to starve yourself."

"Whatever. I have me under control. I've just had a stomach bug for a while and it's caused me to lose weight in the past couple of weeks. Nothing to fret over." Kim mustered up a daring look at them as she took a sip of water, hoping to divert their attention elsewhere.

Darius stood nearby listening and quietly observing Kim as the women brought up the point about her weight loss. He had noticed, too. Whenever he asked her about the rapid shift in her weight, she quickly dismissed him and suspended his thoughts as she made him reach sexual peaks he never did with any other woman.

Kim noticed Darius's unnerving stare and spoke up, directing her attention back to Renee seeing as though everyone else seemed to be still waiting on her to say something. "Sissy, so what the food looks good." Kim couldn't even bring herself to elaborate on how good she knew the food was given that each of them could throw down in the kitchen. Her lack of appetite kept her from enjoying any of it. "I just have to scale back and make better food choices to keep this svelte figure of mine." She didn't even bother to stand up and do her signature spin and frame her silhouette with her hands since she felt another coughing bout coming on. She stood up and rushed to the bathroom. This time she knew she had to vomit the little food that she had eaten.

"That girl is a mess," Monica said as she dropped her cloth napkin on the table and then folded her hands under her chin and stared at Pam. Long and hard.

Pam smirked looking back at Monica. "Don't start with me."

"Oh, you deserve everything we say to you. I can't believe you two eloped." Monica feigned a pout. "We made a pact back in elementary that the four of us, you, me, Renee, and Kim, would be in each other's weddings. You were one of my three maids of honor when I married Keith. I wanted to be in yours and share in that special day with you," Monica said as Kim slipped back in her seat trying to go unnoticed. Monica turned her attention to Renee. "Missy, you better not pull a stunt like Pam. I better be at and in your wedding."

Renee's face scrunched in confusion. "A wedding? I'm not even in a relationship, let alone headed for marriage."

Andrew Dodson, Renee's friend she invited to the dinner party, cleared his throat loudly, intentionally drawing attention to himself.

Everyone else in the room laughed seeing Renee oblivious to Andrew's humorously quasi-offended stance on her statement. Seconds went by before Renee turned her head to see where everyone's laughter spurred from. She stared at Andrew as he looked on to her with his eyes wide and head cocked to the side. "What?" she finally said to him.

"So what am I, chopped liver?" he said through a low chuckle.

"Oh whatever. You know we're not a couple. I was just stating facts and trying to assuage my best friend. She was talking like I was head over heels in love with someone and one step away from opening up a church door and marching down an aisle to say I do." Renee bit her lip as her stomach carried on as if it were the gymnastics portion of the summer Olympics. Andrew's intense stare of her always did that to her. She tried to sit through it but her resistance was no match for the sincere adoration his eyes held for her. She turned her head back to Monica, grateful that her dark complexion masked her heated cheeks. "Trust me, when I get married, you all will be at my wedding."

Monica looked to Kim and barely had her mouth open before Kim stifled whatever she was about to say. Kim raised her hand in protest. "Nope. No need to direct your attention or comments to me about a wedding or anything closely related to it. I'll say this for the umpteenth time, I, Kimberly Denise Williams am never getting married. End of discussion."

Monica opened her mouth to speak, but Kim squashed her potential statement with a daring stare.

Darius merely looked at Kim trying to gauge her body language versus the declaration she made. He saw that they matched. He was okay with that, because while he was growing fonder of her the more time they spent together, they were just alike in that he never planned to get married. *I guess that's why I like her so much.* He put his long neck beer bottle back up to his mouth and took a sip.

Monica laughed as she shook her head and turned her attention back to Pam. "I just can't believe you two though. Why the rush? I'm an event planner. If you wanted something quick and small, I could've easily made that happen for you two."

Pam looked at Monica. She could see that her best friend was truly hurt not being able to share in her special day. "Mon, I swear it wasn't to slight any of you." She turned her attention to Renee and Kim as well. "Look…" She paused, wondering whether or not she should be totally honest. She knew she could do that with the sisterhood and Keith, Renee and Kim's triplet brother, who years back—after secretly pining for Monica for a long time—courted her and became her husband. She was cool with Keith, but still, she never shared her secrets and deep thoughts with him, either. There were others in the room that gave her pause, like Vance's brother and sister-in-law, Marcus and Tameka Sutherland, along with another one of the guys that was like a brother to the other men in the room, Anthony Parham and his wife, Brandy. And then there was Darius Tolliver, Vance's friend and Kim's latest bedmate. She chuckled to herself before speaking up again. "Oh shoot, I'm grown. I'll just be upfront with y'all. The temptation between us to abstain from sex until we were married was just too much for either of us."

The room erupted with laughter. Well, everyone except for Renee. Her prudish ways never afforded them the chance for her to join in on risqué topics with them.

Pam looked at Renee. "Don't look at me like that. You should be happy that we didn't wanna sin but decided to marry."

"What? I'm not judging y'all," Renee said.

"You better not be." Pam laughed and looked down the table at Kim.

"Hey, you know I don't care if y'all did it before or after. You know I believe in living life to the fullest." Kim looked over to Darius who had a sly grin on his face. She winked at him.

Renee shook her head at the exchange between the two bedmates.

"So." Kim laughed staring back at Renee.

Monica interrupted the exchange between the sisters and shifted the room's attention back to Pam. "Even if that was the case, I still could have planned something simple for us all to attend."

Pam cocked her head to the side and stared at Monica. "Really? You, simple?"

Pam, Renee, and Kim laughed at Monica. The four of them had been best friends since middle school and had been extremely close ever since then. Even so that Renee and Kim's mother, Mrs. Williams, specifically called them a sisterhood and encouraged them to stick together and support one another no matter what. That's just what they had done over the years.

"What?" Monica was honestly confused by their merriment.

Kim desperately wanted to clue Monica in on why they were laughing, but she was weak and knew if she opened her mouth, out would come another cough. No words. Just a cough. She acquiesced the floor to Pam.

"Mon, you don't know simple, honey."

"Yes, I do." Monica braced her hands on her hips as she stared at Pam.

Keith chuckled. "No you don't, babe."

"Remember the party you planned for Keith, Kim, and Renee's sixteenth birthday?"

Monica dropped her head and covered her face in shame. Her hands muffled her speech. "Please don't share that story."

"Oh no, please do," Darius said, laughing as he walked closer to the table. "It just may be some new material for my stand-up act. Maybe I can even debut it at the comedy club Saturday night."

Everyone laughed except for Monica.

"Oh no, I'm gonna tell it to help refresh your memory." Pam stood up from the table to better illustrate her storytelling.

Monica kept her head low once Pam took her seat after she finished detailing the story of how

Monica solicited donations from everyone in the neighborhood to get the money to fund the triplet's party. She had placed an ad in the newspaper for the party, went to her local alderman office requesting that the famous Jessie White Tumblers of Chicago perform their act at the party, and even went as far as writing to the Mayor's office and inviting him to the party. All of which she claimed would add variety to the crowd and would look good on her resume for future events she planned.

The continued laughter around the room let her know just how tickled everyone was by the beginning years of what would become her passion, her foundation as an event planner. She brought her head up from her hands and stared at Pam. "Okay, I get your point. I may not have planned such a small wedding for you after all, but, you can't blame a girl for wanting to create a magical moment for a few of her dearest friends."

Pam smiled as she interlaced her fingers with Vance's and looked into his onyx-hued eyes. "It was magical. The only thing that mattered to us that day was becoming one in the sight of God. Him being there made it the best day ever for me." She leaned in and lavished a kiss on Vance that rivaled any other kiss they had shared that night.

Pam couldn't help but to see everyone's eyes zeroed in on her and Vance as they came up for air from their kiss. She wiped her lip gloss from his mouth before looking back at Monica. "Don't give me that look with the way you and Keith go at it at times in front of us."

Monica giggled as Keith pulled her in closer to him while planting kisses on her neck. "That's right. I've loved this woman ever since middle school and I ain't afraid to show it," Keith said before turning Monica's face to his and serenading her with a ravenous kiss.

Renee looked away from the bold public display of affection while Kim smirked and said, "Um, can you two hold off on kissing until Renee and I leave? Y'all know we don't wanna see y'all going at it like that."

Monica kept her face near Keith's and with a sly grin and a hint of humor in her eyes leaned past him and said to Kim, "You'll be alright. We're all grown." She then leaned back into Keith cementing her lips to his.

Renee, not wanting to witness any more of the PDA going on around her, cleared her throat and said, "Pam, while I'm glad you decided to do the right thing and get married before you two sinned, I'm with Monica, we wanted to be at a beautiful wedding for you."

"Ladies, and any gentleman in the room that may not agree with what we did." She looked around at Vance's friends and brother who all held their hands up in surrender as if to say, "no complaints here" propelled her to speak on. "Again, we know you all hate you weren't there but we honestly were focused on the health of our marriage rather than the tradition of a formal ceremony to suit everyone else's desires."

Kim seemed to have her coughing under control as she chose to speak up. "Okay, we forgive you and we can move past the issue, but what I really wanna know is how did your momma, Ms. Eilene, handle the news that you went off and eloped in the midst of all the extravagant planning she was doing for the wedding of her only daughter?" Kim's eyes widened as a new thought occurred to her. "And how did your daddy take not be able to walk his coveted baby girl down the aisle? Oh, you're dirty. Tsk. Tsk." Kim wagged her finger at Pam with a judgmental smirk on her face.

Before Pam could even address Kim, Kim's mouth flew open again. She was acting like her normal self for the moment. "Did you even ask her daddy for his daughter's hand in marriage?" Kim looked baffled at Vance.

Seeing as though Vance was the principal at the school both Pam and Kim were teachers at, he was all too familiar with her brazenness and chuckled before he responded to her. "Yes, I did. He and I had that talk the first time Pam introduced me to her parents. He said he knew I was good for his daughter and gave me his blessing even though Pam and I hadn't brought up marriage with him at all."

"And y'all know my momma, Ms. Drama Queen. Of course, she went ballistic when we told her. She's calmed down a little since the initial shock of it all has worn off some. She said she won't fully forgive me until I give her at least two grandkids from the union."

The sisterhood all laughed knowing how bold and in your face Pam's mom really could be.

"Just like Momma will get over me eloping, so will you all. We're here to celebrate, so let's do just that. No more whining about..."

Pam's words trailed off in Kim's mind as she sat at the end of the table away from everyone else. She was trying her best to be her usual feisty life of the party self, but the gnawing suspicion as to why she had been throwing up and feeling so sick lately numbed her ability to enjoy herself.

2

Kim was in the battle of her life. Her normally high sex drive was low and that infuriated her.

"Not tonight. I'm tired," Kim said into her phone after closing her front door. She'd made it home from the post-wedding dinner at Monica's. She had already told Darius before they left the dinner that he couldn't come over but her rearview mirror proved he hadn't taken heed to her declaration. His slow tailgate behind her landed him outside of her house. She ignored him, smiling as he sat curbside in his car waving at her with that sexy grin of his as she made her way into her house.

He had just the right amount of give and take to him. He wasn't so obtrusive that he would barge his way into her door, yet he knew from times past, him waiting outside of her house to be allowed in always yielded them pleasurable outcomes.

"Let me come in and take care of you. We don't always have to do it when we see each other. Let's just enjoy each other's company," Darius pleaded.

Kim was despising him more and more by the moment. The war zone in her mind and the queasiness in her body was wreaking havoc on her. She hated that it was taking this big of a toll on her, but she wasn't ready to give up what meant freedom to her just yet.

"Just give me a few minutes and I'll let you in." She rushed to her bathroom and opened her medicine cabinet. She pulled the bottle of B12 pills from the shelf and stared at the directions. Although she already knew how many to take at one time, she'd need more than the recommended dosage to satisfy Darius and to help take her mind off her troubles. She was never bored with Darius, but with the reoccurring bout of symptoms, she didn't know if she'd perform with him as she did in the past.

She normally wore a racy outfit when greeting him at the door, but as lethargic as she was, he would have to settle for the matching leopard print bra and panty set she wore.

She freed herself of her clothes, leaving them in a trail behind her as she made her way to the front door. She was about to grab her phone and tell him he could finally come in, but the soft rap at her door let her know he beat her to the punch.

She opened the door and pasted the best smile she could on her face.

He smiled back at her with a glare of concern in his eyes. "What's wrong?" He stepped in, closed the door with his foot, and wrapped one arm around her back pulling her body flush to his.

"Nothing."

"You don't think that I can read you by now?"

"No. I keep telling you, this between us is just what it is, sex." Kim placed her hands on his chest as he lifted her on her tippy toes to smother him with kisses.

With one hand braced at the small of her back and the other gently massaging the nape of her neck, he stared into her eyes.

Kim tried to pull away from him but he held on tightly to her.

Darius had been looking at her the way he was now the past couple of times they were together. That slow perusal of his eyes that said he wanted more than sex with her, he wanted her. But it couldn't be. Not the Darius that admitted he was just like her when they first hooked up, the noncommittal type. She molded her body close to his and ran her tongue across the seam of his lips. She could tell his resistance was fading. The moment her hand pulled on his ear, his weak spot, was the moment the look in his eyes was replaced with lust.

He cupped her butt and lifted her until her legs wrapped firmly around his waist. He planted supple kisses on her neck as he made his way down the hall to the back of her house to her bedroom.

"What the..." He pulled away from her lips to look at what made him stumble upon entering her room. Her normally immaculate room was cluttered with clothes and ungraded papers. After slowly scanning the mess that was her room, he looked back at her. "What's wrong? Your room never looks like this."

The pills had fully kicked in. She had energy. "Shut up and get back to business," she demanded as she kissed his neck and began to rip his clothes off him.

Despite his concern for why she'd let her room look like it did, he gave into her demand. It had been a while since he touched her. He missed her. Some might say that two weeks wasn't long, but two whole weeks without Kim was like a million years to him. He craved her.

With her legs still locked around his waist, he used his arms to clear the clutter on the bed and crawled onto the king-sized haven with her still attached to him. He laid her down and stared at her, treasuring the beauty that was her.

Her lingerie definitely complemented her caramel skin. Even though she was a lot thinner than what he was used to on her, she still was meaty enough to him in all the right places. His slanted, chestnut eyes locked with her dark brown doe-like eyes as he laid her down on the bed.

His tongue laved her navel as his hands danced up her silky skin until he was able to cup her breasts. He felt her tense up. When he looked up at her, the half-smile on her face helped him redirect his attention back to trailing kisses along her stomach. His mouth slowly made its way up to her breasts.

He kissed everywhere but her breasts hoping to heighten her desire for him since he knew she loved that act the most. He pushed his hands up under her and unsnapped her bra. When his hands came from under her, so did both sides of her bra. He pulled each of her arms through the straps and tossed it over the bed where she had discarded all of his clothes.

Smiling and staring at what he thought were the most perfect mounds of breasts, he scaled back from her and allowed his mouth to cover one nipple as he tweaked the other with his fingers.

She squirmed under him.

He thought it was an invitation to continue his sensual attack on her breasts so he sucked and pulled harder until she screamed and shoved him off her as best as she could.

His eyes widened in confusion as he stared at her. "Kim. What's wrong? I thought you liked what I was doing," he said, hunched on his knees and hands hovering over her.

She was horny and ready to let him please her, but no amount of pain pills she had taken eased the awful tenderness in her breasts.

He continued staring at her. She looked as if she was trying to figure out what to say next.

He rolled over on the side of her and pulled her into him as the frown on her face etched deeper into her mouth.

Thankfully, he couldn't see her face as her head lay on his chest.

"You gotta tell me what's wrong, Kim. Normally you love the way I handle you in bed, but just now, that piercing scream of pain and those tears forming in your eyes lets me know something ain't right."

I knew it! I knew he was starting to like me more than what we agreed to. That aching concern in his voice and the way he's holding me now, I can't let him get too close to me. She tried to pull away from him, but he somehow managed to keep a firm yet gentle hold of her.

After seconds of wrestling and trying to get free from him, she was drained. She stopped fighting him.

"You done now?" He chuckled before kissing the top of her head. "Kim, talk to me."

Always quick on her feet, a comeback hit her just like that. "It's nothing, Darius. They just get real tender after my period. This time was worse than any other. Can we just get back to what we were doing? Or, you can leave." She hoped he would choose door number one since she relished in the way he treasured her body. She wanted to, needed to be intimate with him. She needed to remain in control of her body and it not control her.

"You know I don't want to leave." His fingers feathered up and down her arm.

"Okay, then. So let's make it do what it do." She barked at him.

He laughed. "Listen here woman, you don't scare me." He pulled his arm from around her and guided her on her back, and then stretched his body over hers. He kissed her neck as his hands slid in between her thighs. She squirmed under him again.

He lifted off her and braced himself on his forearms on both sides of her. "What's wrong now?"

She cursed under her breath at the look in his eyes. It wasn't annoyance at her squeamishness, but pure concern oozed from him for her discomfort.

She hit his shoulder. "I said they're tender so you can't put your full weight on me."

"Oh." His eyebrows raised, wondering how they would proceed. If she couldn't handle his weight on her then their session would in no way mirror or top any time they'd done it before. "If it's that uncomfortable for you then maybe we shouldn't do it at all."

Kim's eyes widened as she sat up, looking at him. "What?"

He gripped her shoulders and kneaded her tense muscles as he straddled her lap and looked down into her eyes.

"Kim, it's okay. We don't only have to have sex when we're together. We can just lay here and talk or go in the living room and watch a movie."

That same concern he'd shown in his eyes earlier was apparent as Kim looked up into them, but this time it was even more endearing than before. She couldn't afford to let him get any closer to her. Giving her body to him was one thing, but her heart? Never. And she had no intention of accepting his. "The thrill is gone. It's time for you to go. You know the drill." Kim pulled herself away from him and rolled out of bed as best as she could. She found her robe and draped it over her body as he stared at her in shock.

"What?"

She gazed at him, head tilted to the side and lips tight together, unashamed, as if her abrupt leave from the bed was commonplace.

"Really, Kim? You'd think by now you'd be okay with us spending the night with each other."

"Nope. We each made our intentions clear from the beginning." She threw his clothes at him that he'd tossed on the floor earlier.

"Kim, don't do me like this."

"You'll live." She pulled on his arm and helped him out of the bed.

"But...but..." He was at a loss for words as she literally pushed him out of her room and down the hallway towards her front door.

He had finally gotten his shirt over his head when he turned around to face her. "Kim, what's up with you?"

Again, that sweet concern in his voice charged her to remain firm in her stance with him.

"Nothing. You gotta go." She opened the door and ushered him to the other side of it.

He turned to face her again and speak but she slammed the door in his face.

She leaned her back against the door and squeezed her eyes tight trying to subdue the emotions welling in them. *Stop it! Now, out of all times is not the time to let your guard down.* She folded her arms at her chest as she took a deep breath, but immediately dropped them as she winced and began to shake her head. The tears started to fall. Not because of Darius changing up on her, but because of the reoccurring issue that turned her brazen in the first place.

3

Sam closed the door after peeking in on her daughter, Brianna, playing on her tablet. It was a Saturday evening and she had just come in from doing a double at work. She should've been rushing to the bathroom to shower and get out of her nursing scrubs but all she could manage to do was drag her feet to her couch and collapse. She was hungry, her feet and back ached, and she was lonely.

She sighed thinking on how even though she didn't have any family she could depend on and enjoyed being around, she had her best friends, Myra and Trice, who she'd known since high school. They'd been the ones to help her through the highs and lows of her life. Just like when they refused to let her forgo her dream of becoming a nurse when she had fallen in love and gotten pregnant by Brian in undergrad.

While Sam was overjoyed to work in her dream field, she didn't have the happily ever after she thought she would at that point in her life. Days like this reminded her that she was alone. There was no one there to ask her how her day was or rub the tension out of her neck. Brian wasn't an option for her, but she thought she had something special with Darius, but he proved her wrong. And that troubled her day in and day out. *Where did we go wrong?*

She picked up her phone and scrolled Facebook checking her newsfeed.

She smacked her lips reading Brian's posts bragging on the birthday party he and his wife threw for their daughter, Bianca, earlier that day. "You have more than one daughter!" she screamed with her phone close to her lips as if she was screaming in his face. "You always post about your time spent with her, but I bet you won't blast on here how you never spend time with Brianna, will you?" Sam hit the couch before resting her forearm on her forehead. "What did I ever see in him?" She asked herself the question knowing the answer. His smile, his status.

He was a senior when she first started college. One smile from him as they stood in line in the cafeteria and that was it. Before she knew it, they were dating. His attentiveness was so unlike the boys she had dealt with before him that he sent her head over heels in love with him. He had goals and ambitions that he was working toward, rather than the phonies she had dated in the past trying to wow her with plans of grandeur but never acting on them. He said and did all of the right things for the year they were together until she told him she was pregnant. He didn't give her the typical, "Whose baby is it?" response, but his actions showed how he really felt about her and their baby. He became distant with her, claiming that his studies and internship was demanding all of his time.

Her pregnancy was tumultuous, leaving her nauseous and tired all of the time. That reality was compounded by her having to juggle a full-time job and a full class load. He didn't tell her to her face, but she found out through a mutual friend that he had accepted a job in Houston after he graduated. Just like that, he was gone, leaving her to deal with birthing and raising their child alone.

She was a wreck after having the baby. Struggling to balance work and school schedules mixed in with the overwhelming task of being a single parent to a newborn, she battled depression at times. Having enough of caring for Brianna on her own, she got his home address from a mutual friend and flew to Houston with the baby to confront him. But the surprise she experienced jolted a spark of life back into her.

She made the journey years ago thinking that he clearly hadn't gathered how precious the life was that they created together. She thought maybe once he saw Briana, he'd fall in love with her as she did when the doctors first laid her daughter in her arms, but that wasn't the reality she experienced. He didn't coo, wink, or smile when she showed up at his doorstep cradling the baby. One thing was for sure, he couldn't deny that the baby was his. She looked exactly like him. From the same hairy eyebrows to the pointy ears. She remembered the conversation that had played out close to a decade ago as if it had just happened moments ago.

She rang the doorbell and he soon opened his front door. "Sam, what are you doing here?" he asked with a creased forehead.

"Brian, I came to show you your baby, Brianna."

He took a deep breath, stepped out on his porch, and closed the door behind him. He folded his arms at his chest before he spoke. "I got your messages, but..."

"But what?" Sam's voice pitched higher.

"I can't do this right now with you, Sam," he said through tight lips.

"What do you mean, you can't do this now?" Sam pulled her newborn closer to her and inched closer to Brian.

"I just can't. My job requires a lot of my time." He sighed. "I have so much other stuff on my plate." He rubbed his forehead.

"So you're saying you can't be a dad, but you had no problem having unprotected sex with me all of the time? You said it was better that way. Made us closer. You said you loved me." Sam's voice broke.

Brian dropped his head and massaged his temples with the pads of his thumbs.

"You said you wanted a family."

Just then the door to his house opened behind him and he cursed under his breath.

"Brian, what's taking you so long with the delivery man? I'm hungry." A petite, cheery woman stepped out from behind him. "Hello." She stared curiously at Sam. "Who's she?" She looped her arm with Brian's as she leaned into him.

"Nobody, baby. Go inside. You know the doctor has you on bedrest. You're due any day now."

Sam was nauseous. Her eyes welled with tears as she tried to make sense of the scene in front of her. Had the baby not stirred in her hands reminding her she was holding her, she might have dropped her as her body went numb. Muscle control was almost a foreign concept for her, but she soon swallowed her tears to speak. "Nobody? I'm a nobody? She's a nobody?" She rocked Brianna. "You didn't have time to be there for me while I was pregnant and now be a father to our baby, but you have time for her?" Sam's eyes bucked in the girl's direction.

"Look, Sam—" Brian exhaled.

"Brian, what is she talking about?" Brian's girlfriend said as she stepped back from him with both hands on her hips.

He instinctively turned to her. "Baby, I can explain." He placed his hands on her protruding belly, but she smacked them away from him.

He turned a frustrated stare to Sam and said, "Why'd you even come here?"

"Because you've never called me back. I need help, Brian. I need help with her. Brianna needs her father."

Melissa's knees buckled and she grabbed the railing nearby for support. Brian reached out to help her but she shoved him away from her. "Brianna? You have a child I knew nothing about and her name is Brianna. The name we picked out for our little girl. The name we have painted across the wall in bright pink letters in the nursery?" She leaned back against the rail again for support.

"Melissa, babe, you're red which means I know you're heated. Please go back inside and lie down and I'll explain everything to you in a minute."

"No. I wanna know now what's going on, Brian." She winced and rubbed her belly.

He jumped over to her. "You okay? Please, babe, go inside and lay down. You know what the doctor has said about your health now."

"I said I'm not moving until I get some answers," she said through clenched teeth.

He took a deep breath and let out a loud sigh as he rubbed his forehead slowly. He looked at only Melissa as he found the nerve to talk again. "We only dated for a minute in college, but that's been over. I love you. You're my world." He cupped her elbow before she pushed him away again.

"We just dated?" Sam walked closer to the battling couple. "Brian, we were inseparable before I got pregnant with Brianna. You pursued me. You told me you wanted a life with me, to marry me. Brian, you know you were my first." Crying, she punched him as hard as she could.

Melissa gasped.

"Brianna was not a mistake. We never used condoms. You were old enough to know the possibilities. You said you wanted me to be your wife."

Frustrated, Brian shouted, "I lied, Sam. I lied."

Sam took a step back as her eyes widened. "But why?" Her voice was barely audible as she swallowed her emotions.

"You're just too needy, Sam. Too needy." With her slumped shoulders, trembling lips, and tears streaming her face, he saw just how broken she was at his admission. He tried to better explain himself. "It was cool between us at first. I even thought I loved you, but you just became so needy. Demanding so much of my time, so much of me that I couldn't take it anymore. Me meeting Melissa on one of my visits here for my internship and getting the job here was the best thing that ever happened to me." He turned soft eyes to Melissa. "From the moment I met her, I realized what I had with you wasn't real. I found love when I found Melissa. I couldn't be there for you, because I wanted a life with her."

Melissa, wide eyes full of shock, wiped at her tears.

Sam stomped around Brian and slapped him in his face. She walked back to her rental car before he or Melissa could say anything else.

Brianna running in the living room and jumping on her lap brought her out of her reverie. "Mommy, can I spend the night at Ashley's house tonight?"

Sam pouted as she wrapped her arms tighter around her lanky nine-year-old daughter. "So you don't wanna spend your Saturday night with me?"

Brianna giggled. "We're always together, Mommy. Can I please go over to Ashley's?"

"Okay. Go pack your bag while I call Ashley's mom and see if you can."

"I already did. See." Brianna showed her mom the text message from Ashley's mom saying she could come over.

Sam had to push back vile thoughts of Brian as she stared at Brianna smiling with the same measured gap he had. She stared at her daughter, realizing that with the exception of her long ponytails, she was the spitting image of him.

She kissed her daughter's cheek and shooed her to her room to get ready.

She dropped her head in her hands, remembering her long and tough journey of recovering from Brian abandoning her and Brianna. Since her trip to Houston when Brianna was just a newborn, he still hadn't seen her. Sam worked her way back from depression, taking care of her daughter, graduating from college, and then working as a registered nurse. She dated here and there before meeting Darius, but they all seemed to be the noncommittal types, or at least didn't want anything serious with her.

His upfront and straight to the point personality was a stark contrast from Brian, that along with his delectable physical traits had her craving him. He let her know from the beginning that he wasn't necessarily looking for a relationship, but with the way he made her feel when they were together, Sam had easily fallen in love with him. To her, it was only a matter of time before she convinced him that she was the one for him. He had ended things with her a year or so ago, but that didn't matter to her. She'd work to get him back. "I didn't fight for Brian, for my family, but I'm not cowering when it comes to getting Darius back." She smirked.

In her eyes, men like Darius, sure of themselves, educated, charming, and honest were hard to come by. That's the kind of man she wanted in her life and why she had to find out why he ended things with her. "Brianna's going to a sleepover and I'm gonna go down to the club to see if I can get him to come back and sleepover."

4

"Man, I tell you about these ladies with these broomstick bristles for eyelashes." The crowd erupted in laughter as Darius stood on stage performing his comedy act. "I saw this woman one day..." Darius couldn't help but think how beautiful Kim was without makeup. Although she had been wearing more as of late, she didn't do the fake eyelashes and even still it wasn't caked on her skin, it just merely enhanced her natural beauty.

He battled finishing his set as he looked out into the audience to see his buddies all with their ladies and yet Kim wasn't there. She would've blended in well with his group of friends because now her best friend, Pam, was married to one of his best friends, Vance. Marcus was there with his wife, Tameka, and so was Anthony and his wife, Brandy. They'd even got the quietest one of the sisterhood, Renee, to come out with her friend Andrew. But his Kim wasn't there. "Thank you, ladies and gentleman. Enjoy the rest of your night." Darius handed the host the mic and left the stage.

"Ladies and gentleman, give it up again for the hella funny-looking Darius." The room rumbled with laughter as the host told jokes in between calling up the next comedian.

"Yeah, whatever, "Darius mumbled under his breath and smirked as he walked towards his friends table. "What's up, y'all." He dabbed fists with the fellas. "Ladies." He gave them each a head nod. "I'mma head over to the bar and get me something to drink." He quickly left the table in search of something strong to squash the dismay he was feeling. Kim wasn't there.

It wasn't supposed to bother him since he was equally on board with their casual fling from the beginning. In fact, he loved meeting a woman like Kim who saw things the way he did, no strings attached. But somewhere along their tryst it seemed as if emotions got tangled up over her. Like each encounter with her connected a string from him to her and they were weaving closer together to form a bond that he couldn't easily loose himself from. Did he even want to?

He was a social drinker but he wasn't feeling social, but a drink was just what he needed. He walked up to the bar and wedged himself between two couples. One guy looked back and patted him on the back. "You are one funny dude."

"Thanks," Darius said to the guy and then tapped the bar summoning the mixologist.

"You're more than funny, you're sexy. You're amazing..." A slender woman's words trailed off as she leaned in closer to Darius. Normally a woman's breath near his ear like that would send him and her off to a secluded spot to give her what he knew she was subtly asking of him, but this woman didn't evoke that idea in him. She wasn't Kim.

"The usual," he quickly said to the bartender who stood by patiently and smirking as the honey brown beauty flirted with Darius.

Darius finally turned to face the body overcrowding his personal space. "Sam."

"Why so short with me, Darius?" He had been snippy with her the past few times she'd seen him but she wouldn't let his change of heart deter her. She knew he was the one for her.

He let out a long, slow sigh as he put his shot glass up to his mouth. The dark liquor swished in the glass before it touched his lips. He finished it in one gulp and turned to face her. "How are you?" What would normally be a sincere greeting to anyone else lacked the sentiment coming from him to her. It irked him that she still hadn't gotten the clue that what they had was really done with. But being a gentleman, he made small talk with her.

Granted, he had told her some time back that he just wanted to be friends with her, but because he never fully dismissed her when they talked, filled her with hope that she could reclaim his attention. That they would continue on with the future she had planned out for them. One that included them being married, him helping her to raise her daughter, and giving him a junior.

She backed up just enough to look into his eyes and said, "So how have you been?"

"I've been good."

"I can see." Her eyes roamed his body as she slowly licked her lips.

He let out a frustrated sigh and tapped the bar again signaling the bartender.

Chip made his way right over. "Another?" Chip gave Darius a knowing look and chuckled as he readied the drink.

Chip was poised to say something else to Darius when Vance, Marcus, and Anthony approached the bar.

"D, you alright?" Vance said as his hand rested on Darius's shoulder.

"Yeah, man." He tilted his head back and quickly consumed the contents of the shot glass. He clenched his teeth and hissed as the liquid burned his chest. Chip must have made it a double.

He looked to the left of him to see that Sam was still standing there practically fawning over him. "Sam, it was nice catching up with you." His head titled to the side and his mouth curved as if saying to her, "Move along."

She continued to stand there staring at him. It wasn't until his eyes darkened with disdain that she decided to back up from him. "See you soon, Darius." She slowly moistened her lips with her tongue and traced the collar of his shirt with her finger as she brushed past him.

The room was even more crowded than before and grew louder with conversation as music blared through the speakers while the jazz quartet set up for their session.

The gentlemen fanned out around Darius as the couples who had flanked him earlier vacated the stools they occupied. Vance took one, Marcus took the other, and Anthony remained standing nearby.

"Who was that?" Anthony's baritone voice rumbled amidst the other sounds filling the room.

"Nobody," Darius said as he leaned on the bar and stared into his empty shot glass.

Vance laughed. "She may be no one to you, but judging from the way she was staring at you and refusing to leave your side, you're definitely someone to her."

"I said she's a nobody."

"Aye man, watch your mouth. What if she hears you?" Marcus berated him.

"So." Darius's desire to tread carefully with Sam had faded. He was growing somber by the minute as thoughts of Kim's absence consumed him.

Anthony looked to the right of him to see Sam two stools over at the bar engaged in a conversation with another woman. He leaned into the fellas. "It's pretty loud in here and she looks to be knee-deep in her convo with her friend, so hopefully she didn't hear you."

"I don't care if she did." Darius took back another shot and slammed the glass down on the counter.

Their faces scrunched in wonder as they each stared at him. Marcus chose to speak up first. "Man. What's wrong with you?"

"I'm fine." Darius rubbed his temples as his head rested in his palms.

"Quit lying. For one, you've had more drinks than I've ever seen you have in one sitting. And even though I don't agree with your ho'ish ways—"

"Ho'ish?" Vance chuckled with one eyebrow raised as he stared at his brother, Marcus.

"Yeah, you heard right, ho'ish. Men can be ho'ish, too. You know this man never turns away from the opportunity to bed a woman and yet when one who practically looked like she was ready to give it to him right then and there approaches him, he sends her away. Again, I don't condone your lifestyle, but what's wrong with you? Ready to come back to Jesus?" Marcus said.

Darius side-eyed Marcus as he looked over his right shoulder. "Shut up, man. I ain't never left God. He knows I'm a man and I have needs. He and I have an understanding."

"Yeah, He understands that if you don't repent from what you've done and turn from your wicked ways, you gon' lift up your eyes in—"

"Marcus, not tonight, bruh." Vance shook his head.

"Aiight. I'll leave that alone for now." Marcus shrugged his shoulders.

Darius chuckled. "It's cool. You know I'm used to the right Reverend Bishop Apostle Know It All reminding me about God and how he thinks I ain't living right for Him."

They all chuckled except for Marcus.

"Really, bruh. All those names for me?" Marcus stared at Darius.

"Yeah, Reverend," Darius said to Marcus.

"Look, man. We came over here because you look straight out of it. You just killed up there on stage and yet you're over here looking like a kid whose lunch money was stolen. What's up with you?"

"I'm good," Darius said flatly not looking at any of them.

"Naw, it's something. Have anything to do with the woman you were talking to when we interrupted y'all?" Vance said.

"Naw, he looked like that before she stepped to him," Anthony said.

"I said she means nothing to me. I ain't thinking about her."

"Well, what is it then?" Marcus chimed in.

Vance looked back over at his table and smiled at his blushing wife. He quickly scanned the table to see that everyone was there except for Kim. "I know what's up." Vance looked at Darius as the elevator of his understanding reached the top floor. "You mad that Kim ain't here, aren't you?"

"Yup."

"Probably so."

Marcus and Anthony said respectively.

Whereas Darius would normally come back with a joke to deflect any personal attention away from him and the women he dealt with, he sat there silent as he shuffled his shot glass from one hand to the other.

They knew his silence confirmed Vance's suspicion. Vance let out a sardonic laugh as he slapped Darius on the back. "So not only did you finally meet your match, but it looks like you've met your kryptonite. You've got it bad for her."

Darius didn't look up, but said,. "Vance, mind your business and just go back over there with Pam. Matter of fact, all of y'all go back to your wives and enjoy the live band and just leave me be."

"Wow." Marcus rubbed the hair on his face as he looked on to his dismal friend. "No jokes for Vance saying you've met your match? You've got it bad for her, but that's not a bad thing though. Maybe she is the one for you. Nothing wrong with turning in your player card."

"No cards will be turned in anytime soon. I'm not in love," Darius said.

"Yeah, your mouth is saying you're not, but again, judging from your slumped shoulders, your need to guzzle all of the alcohol in here, and dismissing the chick eager to give it up to you, Kim is that one for you," Vance said, shaking his head as if he knew Darius's inner thoughts.

But it can't be true. I'm not a one-woman man. I don't do love. Naw, it ain't love, she's just the best I've ever had. Yeah, she's smart and hella sexy. Sassy. Too much lip, He smirked. *But I love that about her. Love? Nah, it can't be love. But I damn shole wanna know why she ain't here tonight and why she's been so distant lately. Is she with someone else?* His last inner thought made him grip the shot glass in his hand and slam his other hand down on the countertop. "Chip, make it a double again." He held his glass up to him.

"Whoa, bruh. Calm down. What made you heat up so quickly?" Anthony nudged Darius.

"Nothing," Darius said through clenched jaws. Imagining another man inside of Kim, her screaming out another man's name instead of his, made him guzzle down the shot Chip placed in front of him quicker than it hit the countertop.

"Seriously, D. Ease up on the drinking. You know you can't hold straight liquor anyway," Marcus said.

"For real though, man, we've been boys long enough to know your woe ain't work related. You'd bore us with those details in a heartbeat," Vance said.

Darius relaxed for a moment and chuckled thinking about how the guys always ragged on him whenever he got on them about diversifying their financial portfolios.

"The only time you refuse to talk to us about what you're dealing with is if you have real feelings for a woman," Vance stated matter-of-factly.

Darius shrugged half-heartedly. "What? I ain't never been that into a woman where she's thrown me off my game." He turned back to his empty shot glass wishing it were overflowing with what he needed to help take his mind off Kim.

"Yeah it was only that one woman—"

"Shontay." The other fellas said her name in unison as they each shook their heads.

Darius snarled. "I thought we agreed never to say her name again."

"Sorry, bruh. We know you wanted to marry her, and at the time she thought you were wasting your time pursuing comedy right after undergrad. It's crazy that she left you over that. Her loss though. She's stuck raising her son alone after that loser she left you for got her pregnant and dumped her. But look at you, you're a successful financial manager and you keep a gig doing your comedy," Anthony said.

"Losing her was good for you. You gotta stop letting what happened with her keep you from giving it your all with another woman, the right woman," Marcus chimed in.

"I'm telling y'all, me and Kim just kicking it. Nothing deep there."

"Glad I ain't Ray Charles then. I ain't blind to how you treat her when we're all together." Vance chuckled.

"Exactly. He 'round here acting like we don't know what's what." Anthony laughed as he fist-bumped Vance.

"I saw the way you were looking at her at my wedding dinner. Shoot, it was dang near the way I look at Pam." Vance smirked.

"Yeah, she barely had a cough out before you were by her side with water or just trying to pat her back. The look on your face for her said more than your mouth is willing to right now. You ain't gotta hide how you feel for her." Marcus nodded.

"Whatever, fellas. Okay, so Kim may be on my mind, but not like how y'all thinking." He looked at their raised eyebrows as if encouraging him to continue. "It's just that she's the best I've ever had."

"What, fool?" Anthony gave Darius a disapproving look.

"I'm serious. When we're together, you know, doing it, we connect on levels that I've never experienced with another woman."

"Not even Shontay?" Vance covered his gaping mouth with his hand pretending shock to Darius's admission.

"Nope. Shontay was pre-k compared to the post doctorate courses Kim offers in the bedroom." Darius smirked. "So her distance from me over the past weeks has me wondering if it's already over between us. I ain't in love, just a little upset if I won't be hitting that no more."

"You wish it was just about sex. It's deeper than that with her," Vance stated, knowing his best friend.

"Nah, bruh, you're wrong this time. I just felt like tossing a few back. Now let's get back over to the table and enjoy the rest of this jazz set." *Damn. Are they right?* Darius dismissed his thoughts and was the first to leave the bar, and soon the other guys followed him back to the table to be with their wives.

A lady sitting next to the guys vacated her bar stool and went down to join Sam and her friend. "Girl, I couldn't catch everything they said, but one thing's for sure, his guys believe he's really into the woman he's seeing-sleeping with now. Sam, he just may be off the market for good." The woman smacked her lips and started swaying to the music.

41

Sam sat there brewing. Grinding her teeth, her almond colored hand reddening as she squeezed her wine glass in fury. She figured Darius had to be with another woman to be ignoring her, but if he was really into the woman more than he was ever into her, her plans of happily ever after with him just may be ruined. She couldn't afford to let that happen.

5

It was a Saturday morning and Kim had barely made it through her work week. Being sick was making her sick. She didn't know how much of this charade she could keep up. Her energy was waning day by day no matter how many energy pills she took. Her inquisitive students drained her by lunch time each day and she had to guzzle a five-hour energy drink just to make it through to the end of the school day. Luckily, her ongoing research of medicines and best practices for her issue let her know what to take to keep from dropping weight as quickly as she could've, given her condition. Her condition is what shifted her outlook on life to begin with.

She rolled out of bed and headed to the kitchen to make herself something to eat. Although didn't have much of an appetite, she knew she needed to force the food down to help her immune system as best as she could. What she had been doing was helping her to not look as sick as she reluctantly admitted that she was. There were more lumps in her breast now than there were just the week before when she had to end her almost lovemaking session with Darius. She winced thinking about how tender they were, which caused him to care for her more than he wanted to make love to her. *Love? How can you make love to someone if you're not in love with them?* She shook her head to dismiss her line of thinking as she put her serving of soup in a pot on the stove. *Darius,* she thought as she walked into the living room to find her phone. It was still where she'd left it in her purse on the credenza near the front door. She'd dropped it there when she came in from work the day before. She had headed straight to her room, changed into a nightgown, and crashed in bed until she woke up almost thirty minutes earlier that morning.

She fell back on the couch and looked at all the missed calls from the sisterhood and Darius. She knew everyone was trying to see why she hadn't shown up for his set at the club the night before.

She relaxed her head on the soft, deep purple throw pillow on the couch and pulled her chenille throw over her as she mulled over the reason why she didn't show up last night. *Was it because I was really tired? Even though I could've come in, took a nap, and popped some energy pills, drank some matcha tea, and been on my way to the club. Or, was it because I don't like the attention Darius has been giving me lately? Our talks were basic, leading up to sex, but now he's trying to spend more time with me, unrelated to sex, and he's texting me more throughout the day. They're more than just the salacious flirting we do. I can't let him get close to me, just like I've never let any other guy. And especially not now.* She rubbed her left breast and flinched at the pain of the action. No more doctors, no more surgeries. She was tired of what she had endured since right after college over ten years ago. A tear streamed her face as she thought back to when she first found out. An encounter that changed everything about her.

Although not as prude as Renee, she was definitely not carefree with her body as she had become over the years. But the doctor's diagnosis had changed everything.

Her, Renee, Pam, and Monica all had graduated and were getting settled into their jobs, so it was one of the rare times in their friendship where none of them honestly had time to hang out with one another. Brief phone conversations were the mode that kept them abreast with one another.

One day coming home from work, she experienced a pain she never had before. Her mother's words of taking care of herself replaying in her head, sent her right to the ER that evening. She thought she would get a simple answer to her pain that had seemed to dissipate halfway through the visit with the doctor, but the melancholy look on his face when he came in worried her. He ordered more tests, suggesting to her that the matter was far more serious than what she thought it was. The fact that she wouldn't be leaving the hospital soon alarmed her and prompted her to pray.

One would think that she would have immediately called the sisterhood for support, but being the independent person she was, she wanted to hear what the doctor had to say first before she told anyone else. They took her to be X-rayed and the technician talked her through the procedure of what he was doing. He was unable to answer the barrage of questions she threw at him as to why so many X-rays needed to be taken. They were processed and the doctors returned to the room to go over the results with her. The fact that her initial doctor returned with a "specialist", Dr. Ngyuen, and a resident sent bells off in Kim's head. She demanded that the doctor get straight to the point with her.

"Ms. Williams." He spoke in a low, steady voice.

"Doc, just tell me what's what. Now. Please." Her voice quivered with the last of her statement. She hadn't yet developed into the feisty firecracker of today.

"Kim," he pointed to the X-rays illuminated on the wall, "these small masses are centralized in an area common in breast cancer patients."

Kim's eyes widened as she held her breath at the mention of the word cancer.

"Please try and stay calm. We don't know if they are cancerous, but that's why we need to biopsy them immediately."

Kim exhaled. "Okay, so what do I have to do, Doc, to prove to you that I don't have cancer? I need to get back to my great life." The quiver in her voice didn't match the brave facade she was desperately trying to showcase. She needed God and she needed her girls, but again, she decided she wouldn't tell them anything until she had concise knowledge of what was going on with her.

"Okay, I'm glad you're ready to move forward. And from our consult earlier, I remember you saying you had never experienced the pain that brought you here before, right?"

"Right. That's why it's probably not cancer. Maybe I'm just really gassy and those are air bubbles. My momma always says that gas can be lethal if you don't release it. I can't be passing gas all day up and down those rows with my students." She laughed, trying to lighten the mood in the room.

No one else smiled but her.

"How about I give you time to get someone up here to be with you during and especially after the procedure."

"No, I just need answers now. My best friend is leading a song at her church on Sunday and I need to be there cheering her on. So whatever you need to do, do it so I can be on my way." She laid back on the exam table as if they were going to perform the procedure right there.

Dr. Nguyen went and stood by her side. "Kim, we can't perform the procedure in here. A nurse will be here in a second to prep you and bring you down to the room."

"Well alrighty then. Let's get to it. Come on nurse." Nervous of what was next, she jumped off the table and clapped her hands once as if to summon the nonexistent nurse in front of her. The whole process of waiting to learn what could be wrong with her significantly changed her. She didn't latch on to fear, but rather began to build an impenetrable wall around herself. She began to don the persona of the person she would morph into years later—straightforward and sarcastically vocal. She was getting snippier with people by the moment.

Dr. Ngyuen, the specialist, and the resident left the room. Kim shook her head in shock of what she was soon to experience in hopes of a good report coming from it. Her big doe eyes welled with tears as the mixture of emotions washed over her.

The door opened and she immediately turned her back to the nurse entering so that she could clear her face of the tears that had betrayed her and covered her face.

"Ms. Williams, how are you? Ready to get changed?" The elderly woman's calm voice did nothing to soothe Kim's tattered nerves.

With her back still gracing the nurse, she said, "Yes, I'm ready. Let's do this."

Kim's memory of her first time at the doctor faded as a text message alert caused her phone to vibrate. It was Darius looking to see how she was doing. He wanted to know her whereabouts the night before.

She threw the phone across the room. It landed on another couch. She wiped her tears, remembering Dr. Ngyuen's diagnosis that day after her biopsy over ten years ago. She indeed had breast cancer. Still in shock from the doctor's diagnosis, she missed Monica's performance at church that Sunday blaming her absence on having too many papers to grade before work that Monday morning.

Instead of using the sisterhood, her brother, and her loving parents for the support she knew they would have easily provided for her, the realization of her diagnosis warped her senses and became the catalyst as a call to live her life with no regrets. She resolved that day that she would answer to God at the end of her life for any transgressions committed.

She didn't follow Dr. Ngyuen's advice to have the masses removed immediately as she mulled over whether or not she would tell anyone about her issue.

She woke up one morning realizing she didn't want them fussing over her health issue. She scheduled the procedure to occur the day before Christmas break started knowing she would have two weeks to recover and get back to work and on with her life. What she took as a near death experience birthed a new version of herself. She didn't believe that she forsook God and His divinity. She just simply wanted to live life on her terms and not based on a diagnosis or anyone else's rules for that matter.

But that first dance with cancer wouldn't be her only bout. It seemed like just about every two years, she experienced some type of discomfort or symptom that sent her to the doctor only to find out that she had a new type of cancer somewhere in her body. The second time it was thymus cancer and the third time, it was ovarian cancer. Each subsequent bout was not as progressive as they could've been given they were each caught early.

None of them required intrusive surgery, only quick outpatient surgeries were warranted.

Ironically, she got them at the beginning of the summers and claimed to travel abroad during the summers, but really, she stayed locked up at home with her car out of sight. Doing so allowed her to keep her distance from the sisterhood and her family so they wouldn't see her weak and healing from the minor surgeries and cancer treatments.

One would think that she would reach out to those who loved her for support and encouragement, but that wasn't the case. Each bout only made her exterior roughen all the more to the witty and often callous, in-your-face, and flirtatious Kimberly Denise Williams that people came to know her as.

Getting back to her present-day dilemma, Kim mulled on her couch that Saturday morning with her tears steadily flowing. The lethargy she was experiencing along with the tenderness in her breasts let her know that there was definitely something going wrong in her body. This time she had the morbid feeling that this bout would be way worse than the others she experienced.

6

Kim stood at her front door struggling to put the key in its lock as her tears blurred her vision. "How did I even get home?" she whispered as she swiped away the tears on her face. After she managed to unlock her door and enter her home, she dragged her feet to her kitchen and pulled out a bottle of Cooper's Hawk red wine. She knew it would be her last glass. After the news she had just received from Dr. Ngyuen, wine and a lot of other stuff wouldn't be in her future. Just the thought of what her doctor shared with her forced her to empty the bottle of wine into the tall goblet filling it to its rims.

She didn't turn the lights on when she entered the house, so the stream of moonlight illuminating a sliver of the kitchen was befitting for her. It mirrored her life—darkness. She snarled as her head fell back preparing to gulp as much wine as she could.

She leaned over the countertop remembering Dr. Ngyuen's exact words to her earlier that evening. Despite how she felt, she had put off going to the hospital for two weeks after her last encounter with

Darius, but the pain in her body forced her to make good on attending her appointment after work that day.

She sat in Dr. Ngyuen's office waiting for her to return with the lab results. Kim remembered looking around the room thinking the doctor must've thought her blue color palette for the office would somehow soothe patients as she delivered unfavorable news to them. However, the color choices didn't serve that purpose for Kim. They sickened her. She wished there were vibrant hues of orange and red and yellow around her, encouraging her that she could still remain the fireball that she was all the days of her life. But seeing the deadpan stare in the doctor's eyes as she finally came in and sat next to Kim, let her know things would never be the same.

As usual, Dr. Ngyuen tried to be gentle and ease into telling Kim that her suspicion of a return of cancer in her body was correct, but Kim's short temper egged her to get straight to the point. Dr. Ngyuen gripped Kim's hand into hers and said, "Yes, Kim, it's back."

For some reason, tears streamed Kim's eyes as they hadn't since her first diagnosis. She knew she beat it before, but she just felt differently this time.

Kim used the excuse of needing to wipe her face of her tears as her reason to pull away from the doctor's empathy gesture. "Kim, I've seen the physical toll it's taken on your body, but I can only imagine the emotional one it's taken on you each time. The results show that cancer appears in several regions of your body and unfortunately we didn't catch its progression as soon as the others. I'm certain though, that with your resilient spirit, you'll beat this and be in good health again in no time."

Kim had zoned out near the end of Dr. Ngyuen's speech. Mere head nods were her only response the remainder of the conversation. She heard what her next steps were but she couldn't focus on the drive home. It took all she had in her to see through her tears, and clearly the grace of God, to make it home.

She finally stood up straight next to the kitchen island. She gulped the last of the red wine to drown out her visit to the doctor earlier before she trudged over to her couch and collapsed on it. She balled up in a fetal position and wept the rest of the night cradling her cancer-ridden body.

7

After her doctor's visit and learning of her diagnosis, Kim couldn't bring herself to go to work. She was out of it mentally, and all the tricks she had mastered over the years to hide the symptoms of her cancer and the treatments just weren't working.

Her doctor's appointment had been that Monday. It was Thursday and she hadn't been to work. She hadn't set up her chemo appointments either. She wasn't sure if she had the fight in her this time around. Dr. Ngyuen's promptings of getting the chemo started immediately kept ringing in her head, yet she hadn't made the moves to schedule and start.

Of course, with her and Pam working at the same school, the sisterhood was privy to her absences at work, but her random excuses she had come up with over the years allayed their suspicions. She just hoped they'd do the same this time.

The incessant ringing of her phone zapped her out of her misery induced state of depression long enough to read the screen. It was Dr. Ngyuen's office and she knew exactly what she wanted.

Knowing she couldn't ignore the doctor forever, she answered the call right before it went to voicemail.

"Kim, how are you?" Dr. Ngyuen's Vietnamese accent was no longer as thick as it was over a decade earlier when the two first encountered one another. Kim clearly understood every word she said now.

"Kim?"

"Yes, I'm here." Kim shifted in her bed to a more comfortable position.

"I know you're probably nervous, worried about it being back, but remember, since your cancer is in a later stage than before, it's important that you start chemo, maybe even radiation, right away. Please."

Kim honestly appreciated the doctor's sincerity. She just didn't know if she had the amount of fight in her needed to withstand the amount of radiation Dr. Ngyuen suggested to hopefully eradicate the cancer.

After beating cancer as she had before, most people would marvel in the miracle, but she knew many weren't willing to accept the negative aspect of cancer and its treatment. The treatments did just as much emotional damage to one as it did with obliterating cancerous cells. It was like it somehow managed to burn up levels of hope in Kim. But with the way she was feeling at the moment, maybe the chemo would make her feel better after all. "Can you take me today?"

"Sure. Come in. But Kim, can you not do it alone this time? Before was less invasive than what will be needed now. You'll need your friends and family this time. At the very least someone will have to pick you up from the sessions as you know you'll be drained afterwards." Hope shone in the doctor's voice.

"I'll be fine." Kim was in no mood to involve her family and friends. She'd made her deal with God a long time ago. Either He would heal her or He wouldn't. Either way she wasn't mad at Him. She just figured it was her lot in life for having pre-marital sex so long ago. "Is noon good?"

"Yes. See you then."

Kim ended the call. She wouldn't be hardheaded this time and try to drive herself from chemo. However, she had no intentions of having anyone she knew pick her up. She would simply call an Uber after her appointment.

She peeled herself off the bed and went into the master bathroom to make herself presentable for her appointment. She had a little over two hours to create magic from the catastrophe that was her face when she looked in her mirror. Bags and dark circles hung under her eyes from having cried day in and day out. She knew her current look would be Miss America standards in comparison to what the repeated and intense rounds of chemo could do to her. She may have been out of it spirit wise but she'd hold on to the glamor girl persona she carried over the years as long as she could.

She showered and got out only to stand in front of the mirror again thinking of how pallor cancer patients could look at her stage of the disease. She patted her face and shook her head reflecting on how only minimal damage had occurred to her physical appearance before. And the little damage and surgical scars she experienced were easily covered up with makeup until time erased its remnants.

When she was satisfied with her final head to toe look, she wiped her face again of the ever-present tears before exiting the bathroom. *When have I ever cried this much?* she asked herself as she locked the door behind her.

She looked at her phone to see that the Uber driver was outside of her house. She made her way to the car and barely greeted the driver as she secured herself in the backseat.

She transitioned from staring out the window to looking at the driver as he ogled her. He made no attempt to hide the fact that he liked what he saw when he looked at her in his rearview mirror.

Any other day, Kim would've severed a man's pride who approached her but didn't meet her standards. However, that day, although she wouldn't let him know, she appreciated the mid twenty something brother's assessment of her soon to be diminished beauty.

It might be the last time a man ever found her to be attractive if her post chemo fate was like that of many of the other patients she saw years ago at the treatment center. She didn't even flinch at the faint smell of marijuana lingering in the car. She always drove herself so she had no need for public transportation and taxis. The few times over the course of her adulthood where she chose to take a cab into downtown Chicago rather than pay the absurd prices for parking, she wouldn't get into a cab unless it almost smelled and looked to have come off the assembly line. But the smell of the herb accosting her nostrils had her thinking otherwise.

Although probably an improper move for a teacher to be smoking weed in her off time, if the medicine would indeed help her get through chemo and diminish the decay of her beauty, then perhaps she would talk to Dr. Ngyuen about it being an option for her.

"We're here," the dread-headed driver said, flashing what he must've thought was his winning smile to Kim.

She unbuckled her seat belt and open the car door.

"Wait. Uh, I was wondering if I can get your number." He turned to face her as one forearm rested on the steering wheel and the other one gripped the headrest of the passenger seat.

"Sorry. I'm taken."

"Dude is winning then. Enjoy your day." He smiled at her before turning his trap music up loud and speeding off.

"I'm taken?" Kim said aloud to no one. "Yeah, I'm taken alright, by cancer." She slowly lifted her head to stare at the big building in front of her. Loyola offered the best care when it came to the prominent type of cancer she had.

She reached for her vibrating phone thinking maybe she should answer one of the endless calls she was receiving from those close to her, but that stubborn spirit in her overrode any capacity she had to be comforted by them. "I've done this alone many times before, one more time won't hurt." She let out a loud sigh as her lead heavy feet made their way into the hospital.

8

Kim's first chemo session was Thursday morning and yet there she was lying in bed on a Sunday morning missing church with her family. She knew she would miss the family dinner after church as well.

She was drained. She pulled herself out of bed en route to the bathroom. She stopped short of the toilet and stared at herself in the mirror. She pulled at her face, disgusted by the fact that it wasn't as plump as it had been all of her life. Her pallor skin was not as vibrant as it normally was given the daily regiment she enacted to keep up her appearance. What used to be her big, bright, round, doe eyes were clearly sunken in more so than she had ever seen them before.

Tears welled in her eyes.

She turned her face from side to side as she inched closer to the mirror, leaning over the granite countertop. Her lips curved upward partially taking in the fact that she in no way looked like her normal, glamorous self, but relished in the notion that the marijuana Dr. Ngyuen had prescribed to her and she had been smoking since her first chemo session, admittedly kept her from wasting away as quick as she could have up to that point.

She could hear her phone ringing and knew that it was Renee from the special ringtone she'd given her. She slapped the cold, earth-toned countertop with both open palms as tears finally streaked her face and she stared in the mirror. "When will you tell them?"

Everyone had been calling her nonstop trying to find out why she had gone AWOL on them this time. She shook her head thinking about the conversation that drained the little bit of energy she had the night before.

"Hello."

"Kimberly Denise Williams! What in the light of day is wrong with you?" Renee said frantically.

"Mother Goose, I see you still don't know how to set up a good joke." Kim rolled over on her other side away from the moonlight shining on her.

"I'm with her. Why have you been avoiding us? Monica said worried.

"Yes, why have you?" Pam chimed in.

"Because I'm grown and I can."

"No, you can't. You can't get on us when we get distant from the group and yet you go off on your own and think that's fine," Renee said as if she were the older sister.

"Watch me. Goodnight, ladies." Kim pulled the phone away from her ear willing to end the call but the pleas of her dearest friends and sister to not end the call chipped a little piece of the wall she had erected around her heart.

"Okay, I won't hang up on y'all just yet, but, your time is short. I'm honestly tired, ladies." Kim wrapped her free arm around herself for comfort.

"First off, I wanna know why you haven't been to work the entire week?" Pam asked.

"I already answered that question. I was sick and now I'm with my friend."

"So, it's over with you and Darius?" Monica asked worriedly.

"Nothing ever really started. Don't play dumb. Y'all know what we were getting from each other. No emotional attachments, just sex."

"Well, I can't tell the way he moped around after his set Saturday night over you not being there," Pam said matter-of-factly.

Kim shifted in bed. "You don't know that."

"Yes, ma'am. I do. I saw it with my own eyes how hung up he is over you. And I definitely know from convos with Vance that your disappearing act has Darius all out of sorts."

"I don't know why. He knew from the beginning what we were about. We both laid our cards on the table and liked each other's hands knowing we were playing the same game."

"Everything is not a game, Kim. If the man has feelings for you, there's nothing wrong with that. Despite your brashness and rough exterior, you honestly are loveable, at times." Renee laughed.

"Yeah, whatever. Seriously, ladies, I'm tired and heading to bed now. Good night."

"Wait, don't go yet. When will we see you again? We miss you," Monica said.

"And something ain't right. You're not telling us something. As you say, you've been sick lately and you're too sleepy to talk on the phone with us? Kim 'life-of-the-party' Williams is in bed on a Saturday night and not up mingling. Oh my God! You're pregnant!" Pam gasped before covering her mouth.

"What?" Kim mustered up enough energy to sit up in bed.

"That's what it is." Monica hit the bed as she lay in hers. "You're pregnant with Darius's baby. Does he know?"

"What?" Kim shook her head in disbelief as it fell into her palm. If she wasn't so stunned, she would've laughed at the absurdity of the ladies' line of thinking.

"Oh, sissy, please don't shut us out during your pregnancy. How far along are you? Is it that you haven't shared it with us because you're not sure if you want to keep the baby?" Renee's voice faded in fear.

Kim couldn't get a word in edgewise as the sisterhood bombarded her with one question after the other. Her usually cutthroat demeanor took a backseat to her exhaustion.

"Please don't make the same mistake like me and Renee when it came to hiding the details of our pregnancies back in college. Look how that turned out for us. Me having an abortion had me running away from the love of my life, your brother, thinking

I couldn't give him babies because false reports from the doctor after my abortion. And the fallout from Renee's secret is still unresolved. You remember, she initially told us she had an abortion only to find out recently that she really didn't. She gave the baby up for adoption. She's still not sure if she'll seek him out to build a relationship with him and you know how that's been eating at her," Monica said.

Kim breathed a deep sigh readying herself to speak but Pam spoke up first. "Are you afraid of love, Kim? Think the baby will tie you down to Darius? I know you've always said you don't want kids and that you'll never get married. Having the baby won't be a mistake, having sex before marriage is where we falter. But you know God can turn our mistakes into a blessing if we let Him. This all can work out for your good. I see the way you are with Darius around us. You like him more than just a sex partner. Give him and the baby a chance."

There was a pregnant pause before Kim finally decided to talk. She cleared her throat before doing so. "If I had the energy to right now, I would laugh a mighty laugh at you fools, but since I'm sincerely tired, I'll say that you all are wrong and good night." She hung up the phone despite the various protests from the sisterhood not to do so.

She dropped the phone in front of her as she let her head collapse into her hands. It was no surprise to her that the ladies line of thinking went down the path it did. After all, had it been one of them acting as she was, she probably would've assumed the same. Most often, she was the one that led the interrogation of the others in the past few years with their sketchy behavior. She wasn't mad at them for caring about her, she just didn't need or couldn't take their meddling at the moment, which was why she grabbed her phone again and shut it down as opposed to answering the call from Renee.

She fell back in bed grateful that they didn't dig too much into her whole weekend getaway excuse with an old friend. Of course, it had become overshadowed by their delusions of her being pregnant and that somehow she and Darius just might have a happily-ever-after after all.

A tear seeped from the corner of her eye as she struggled to even her breathing, recognizing another crying fit was about to ensue. *I'll never get a happily-ever-after. It's my fault, though. I made my bed and now I have to lie in it.*

She rubbed her stomach amidst her heaving shoulders and mumbled, "Nope, they'll never be a baby in here. I won't live long enough to see that happen."

She missed being around the sisterhood. She missed Sunday dinners with her family. She missed playing with her niece and nephew.

If she were to be totally honest with herself, she missed Darius. He had been the only man in a long time who, although he never verbally let on, actually seemed concerned with her outside of the bedroom. In fact, he was the only one to ever meet her friends, brother, and sister. Granted, that happened because of his friendship with Pam's husband, Vance, but still, no man had ever been privy to her life outside of sex. Not from a lack of trying on their part, though.

There were many who tried to start something serious with her, but she would shut them down instantly and end things with them altogether. She knew from her first bout with cancer that she could never allow a man to get close enough to her for him to fall for her, let alone for her to remotely mature any emotional attachment to him. Which is why she needed to steer clear of Darius. She sighed. "But I enjoy going to the comedy club on Saturday nights. He really is funny. Besides, the others will be there so I have to go to keep them from prying any further into my life," she said aloud to herself as she snuggled under the covers.

She would smoke all of the weed she needed to and eat as healthy as her appetite would allow her to be in enough shape to go back to work Tuesday. She and Dr. Ngyuen discussed how the marijuana would help with her nausea and vomiting after chemo. She predicted that she would be past the immediate symptoms of her first round of chemo by then.

She knew her return to work would allay some of the sisterhood's worry of her. She would also muster the nerve and strength to go to game night at Pam and Vance's on Friday night and the comedy club on Saturday night. Even though she had chemo again on Thursday and was certain her energy levels would be at an all-time low, she knew showing her face would hush them for the time being.

And as for Darius, she'd figure out how to deal with him when she saw him. She wiped her nose with her sleeve as she cried herself to sleep.

* 9 *

Kim took a deep breath and let out a sigh of relief after receiving only a mild interrogation from the office staff moments earlier. She feigned a smile as they all commented that she must've really been sick seeing as though they could tell she had lost weight. Some jokingly asked if what she had was contagious. Any other time Kim might've coughed on them and riled them to answer their own question in a couple of days just to get a reaction out of them, but she knew she needed to save her energy to make it through the day. She simply smiled and nodded her way out of the office.

Having taught the sixth grade for a little over ten years and the fact that teachers had to submit six weeks worth of lesson plans at a time, she knew what unit and what part of the unit they would be on, so a quick glance at the lesson plan on her desktop put her back up to speed with what she and the kids would have to do that day.

She looked around at vibrant yellow and orange walls, colors she had chosen symbolizing energy, and a tear fell down her cheek wondering how many more times she would get to sit in the room as its teacher before her cancer-ridden body stripped her of the life she knew and the one she thought she would yet experience. More tears fell remembering Dr. Ngyuen showing her the x-rays of how many places masses showed up in her body. After extensive testing, they all proved to be cancerous. That's why Dr. Ngyuen hounded her about starting chemo as soon as possible. Although the doctor had expressed hope, Kim had read so many cases where patients with similar diagnoses didn't survive whether it was caught in its infancy or in its last stages.

The bell rang signaling Kim's tears and pity party would have to stop. She never was one to revel in either of them anyway and besides, she had to prepare herself for the show she was about to put on in front of her students. She reached into her oversized purse and grabbed the B12 bottle and unscrewed the lid as she walked towards the mirror in her closet. By the time she made it there she had popped four 1000mg pinkish pills into her mouth. As she suspected, looking in the mirror showcased her ruined foundation courtesy of her tears. She made a mental note to go to Sephora after work to replace her "sick" foundation. She really only wore makeup during the times she had cancer over the years and needed to masque the effects of it on her face. She hadn't been out of her house since she left her chemo session Thursday so she realized she had long since discarded the dried-up foundation that would have withstood her tears and even blistering heat. Even the most expensive brand at Walgreens, the only store open before heading to work that morning, wasn't the best cover up for the healthy look she was trying to accomplish, but caking it on as she did was her only option. The tears she cried earlier had washed through at least three layers of the creamy foundation and forced Kim to stand in the mirror with a sponge in her hand rushing to smooth over the streaks before the chatty kids she heard in the hall enter her room. Thank God she had waterproof mascara on, otherwise her raccoon-like face would have surely alarmed her students. She raised her forearm to her nose and sniffed herself one more time to ensure she didn't smell what she smoked before she left her house that morning. Grateful that her neighbors couldn't see into her backyard, she wore a sauna suit, shower cap, and plastic gloves as she stood on her patio and smoked. Through trial and error that weekend, she learned the nonporous materials really did help to keep the smell of the cannabis from sticking to her clothes, skin and hair. She undressed at her back door and rushed to shower, scrubbing her body with lemon juice and then soaking in peppermint oil. Over the weekend, she had come to see how the routine really did neutralize the smell.

Chuckling a little at the sight of herself earlier that morning, she turned her head when the door to her classroom opened and in flooded thirty-two students eager to welcome the return of their homeroom teacher.

"Ms. Williams." Many of them screamed as they rushed and huddled her each trying to push another out of their way to hug her.

She smiled and the reality of them having missed her as much as she did them settled into a big lump of emotion clogging her throat. She took a deep breath and counted to ten as she slowly released her breath hoping that by the time she made it to one the appearance of the tears watering her eyes would cease. She was successful. She didn't cry. She merely cleared her throat before speaking, "Hi, y'all. I missed y'all, too." She turned to face them. "We'll catch up in a minute but you all know the morning routine."

"We know," one chubby boy called out.

"You gotta take attendance. It's LaKeisha's week to do the lunch count and we have to get our things ready for the day."

"Exactly, Marquise." She hugged the remaining students around her before urging them to their seats.

People would probably assume that she had a split personality disorder if they witnessed her with adults versus students. She didn't need to pull her sarcasm out and be rough with her kids. She was able to be the kind-hearted person she had always hoped to be before her first bout with cancer, but after it, she felt the need to morph into Ms. Tough.

LaKeisha, Kim's busiest and bossiest student, stood near her desk with a clipboard in her hand checking off the kids in the room. Once done, she made marks on the lunch envelope before attaching it to the clipboard. After that she placed the stack of lunch cards secured with a blue rubber band into the pocket of her snug uniform pants. "Okay, so the lunch count is done and everyone is in their seats and have started on the morning exercise."

"Everyone but you." Kim peered over her grande espresso.

"I know that," LaKeisha clapped her hands, "but that's because I decided to be the spokesperson for everyone."

Kim placed her cup on the table, sat back in her seat, and folded her arms across her chest as her stare narrowed in on Lakeisha.

Lakeisha paused for a moment wondering if she could continue. Kim didn't have to do much to keep her class in line nowadays, because she had asserted herself as a no-nonsense teacher early on in her career. The strict manner in which she operated initially had kids warning their younger siblings years to come not to play around in Ms. Williams class when they finally had her as a teacher. Being that way was worth it for her first years seeing as though she could scale back over the years on the rough exterior with the kids and just enjoy teaching them. Not only did they fear her, more importantly, they respected her and cared for her which is why Lakeisha gulped air and fashioned a smile on her face before continuing on. "Come on, Ms. Williams. You know we care about you. We just wanna make sure you're alright."

The concern in LaKeisha's voice and the concentrated looks of the children pulled heavily on Kim's emotions. She didn't know how she would make it through the day without crying with the love and concern her students were showering on her.

She cleared her throat again before speaking and only looked at Lakeisha. To look at all of them would certainly have sparked the onset of her tears. "Kids, I have been sick, but I'm here now and that's all that matters," Kim said finally scanning the room.

"But you still don't look good."

Kim cursed the cheap foundation on her face.

Lakeisha snapped her neck in the direction of the girl who screamed out the truth to Kim. "Shanita, don't make me hurt you, girl. My teacher ain't never ugly." Lakeisha took off, charging towards her prey but Kim's voice halted her steps.

"Lakeisha, don't you walk any further."

Lakeisha turned back to Kim. "I was just going to check her for calling you ugly."

"She didn't call me ugly. She said I still didn't look good, meaning I don't look like I'm fully over what I had. Right, Shanita?" Kim turned a calm stare to Shanita.

"Yes, ma'am. I would never call you ugly, Ms. Williams. You too pretty for that. I was just saying you still look sick to me."

"I know you weren't calling me ugly, Shanita." She winked at the frightened girl. "And thanks for trying to come to my rescue, Lakeisha, but don't ever try to bully someone because they say something you don't like. Two wrongs don't make a right."

"But she—" Lakeisha raised her hands in protest.

"But nothing. Didn't you just hear what the girl said? And even if she called me ugly, it still wouldn't give you the right to try and intimidate her with your words or your actions. Go sit down somewhere, missy." Kim smiled as she shooed Lakeisha to her seat.

Lakeisha returned a metal braced smile as she finally headed to her seat.

Kim shook her head at the time spent with her kids thus far as she pulled up their assignment to display on the LCD projector. She heard the onslaught of an argument between two kids but before she could even fix her mouth to speak, she could hear Lakeisha reprimanding them.

Lakeisha stood in between the two children at odds and pointed to a conflict resolution chart forcing the kids to look up there, too. "Y'all got a problem, follow the directions to get it solved. Ms. Williams is still sick and don't need to be bothered with y'all silliness." Lakeisha pursed her lips and went back to her seat to get back to her work. The students each studied the chart for some time before they got back to work.

Kim inwardly laughed at the tall, lanky girl as she had swiftly and effectively redirected her peers, but Lakeisha was right, she was tired and still sick. She was grateful that the kids listened to Lakeisha and avoided further arguing. One thing she could say for inner city kids was that when they loved their teacher, they loved their teacher. Moments passed of serenity and soon Kim lined the kids up and took them to art class.

She returned to her room and fell back in her chair knowing she didn't have the energy to do any more prepping for the day than what she'd already done. "Thank God their activities for the day are more self-directed than teacher-led. If this were a lecture day, I would just have to be honest with myself and leave work early."

"Who are you talking to?" Pam asked as she burst into the room.

Kim cursed herself for not locking her classroom door once she returned from taking her kids to their special. She wanted to curse out loud for working at the same school as one of her best friends.

"I don't care about you rolling your eyes over there. I came in here to see you. You're back at work and since you've been avoiding us, I knew now might be the only time to catch you."

"Okay, you see me. Now go away so I can take a quick nap." Kim closed her eyes as she rested her folded arms across her chest.

Pam circled Kim's desk to hover over her. "Sweetie," she put the back of her hand against Kim's forehead, "you don't look like your usual self. The baby is really taking a toll on you, hunh?" Pam sat on Kim's desk.

Forgetting that her best friends thought she was hiding a pregnancy from them, her eyes flew open and she sat straight up to stare at her misinformed friend. The kids' inquiry was child's play compared to the third-degree interrogation that she was sure to get from Pam now that they were face to face. "As I told you all the other day, I am not pregnant. I've just been sick." Kim sat back and closed her eyes again.

"Nah, you're pregnant. If you were sick, you'd tell us. But I do believe a pregnancy would scare the crap out of you because it's not the life you've said you wanted, even though I've always thought you were lying about that, too. What'd your doctor say about these symptoms you've been experiencing? You've gone to the doctor, right? Kim it's very important that you get the best prenatal care. Especially if the pregnancy is making you sick the way you are."

Kim refused to refute Pam's foolish talk. She kept her eyes closed.

"Life is weird, though. Being pregnant can make one woman glow or another's hair grow. Some women carry their babies in every other body part other than their stomachs and some have to go on bed rest early into their pregnancy because they blow up so quickly. You, you've gotten much smaller. Maybe that runs in your family. Renee did say she was able to hide her pregnancy from that abusive jerk Ted back in college because she was barely showing. So, I guess there's no need to be so concerned over you not showing yet. Wait, how far along are you?" Pam paused her rant to stare at Kim as her feet dangled from the desk.

"Will you shut up already." Kim kept her eyes closed. Her mouth was dry so she had no choice but to sit up and grab her water bottle to quench her thirst. She hated that cotton mouth was a side effect of chemo. She replaced the top on her water bottle and then stared at her friend. "I've told you the truth about my appearance, but you refuse to believe me." She stood up.

Pam gasped but immediately covered her mouth.

Kim ignored Pam's reaction and walked to the mirror to see if she had deteriorated any more since she had been to work, if that were possible. But she hadn't. She looked in the mirror to see that her cheap foundation was doing a poor job of upgrading her features.

Pam's knee bounced on the desk as she warily stared at Kim. She slowly lowered herself from the desk and treaded lightly towards her friend. Kim didn't fill out her clothes the way she normally did, and that scared Pam. She knew Kim prided herself on her appearance, how sharp she looked in her clothes. To not see that alarmed her. It wasn't as if the clothes were swallowing her, but for there to be an inch between Kim's skin and the material on her pants, to see her friend usually bright, doe eyes be lackluster, downright frightened her.

She made her way to Kim and draped her arm over one of her shoulders and rested her chin on the other. She looked into the mirror to stare at her friend. "Sweetie, I don't know whatever it is that you're keeping from us, but please share it with us. It looks like it's starting to kill you. We promise we won't judge you about having a baby out of wedlock. And if that's what's stressing you out, then you gotta be healed of that self-condemnation and fear of judgment soon. It's not healthy for you or the baby."

Kim took a deep breath to keep herself from crying. She had been carrying the burden of her illness by herself for so long and had forgotten what it was like to feel the comfort of her friends' concern, but Pam's close proximity to her was sending her emotions in overdrive. She needed to get away from her quick. Otherwise, she just might tell her exactly what was wrong with her.

The bell rang. Kim was grateful for it, too. It meant they both had to go get their students. Kim let out a sigh of relief for a reprieve from Pam's presence. At work was no place to tell one of your best friends that you're dying.

10

Kim walked through her front door, rushed to her couch, and collapsed. It took a lot of work keeping up the semi-energized facade she carried on since returning to work.

Of course, her time spent with Pam in her classroom the day before only made the sisterhood drown her with more questions, but the ability to screen calls and silence the ringer was necessary and heaven sent.

Not only had she been ignoring the sisterhood, but she thought she was doing a great job of ignoring Darius, too. She'd deal with him Saturday night when she saw him at the comedy club and put to rest any ideas he had of them being more than what they were.

She had just closed her eyes when her doorbell rang.

Her eyebrows furrowed as she titled her head to the door looking at it as if the door had offended her. She closed her eyes again and dropped her head back on the pillow.

The doorbell rang again.

"My car's in my garage. No one knows I'm really home. They'll get the picture when I don't open it," she mumbled against the pillow.

The doorbell rang again.

Her neck snapped towards the door and she shot a deathly stare at it, wishing somehow the person on the other side could sense her disdain for their presence.

She curled into a ball hoping to fall into a deep slumber, but the doorbell rang again and this time was followed by knocking.

She shot up from the couch. Her adrenalin to scold whoever was at her door overrode her exhaustion as she stomped to it.

The knocking continued as she made her way to the door.

She snatched it open ready to lay into the assailant but her words were caught in her throat as she stared at Darius. He was downright sexy, even with his jaws clenching as he stared at her.

She could tell he was mad.

Lodged in the doorway, she folded her arms across her chest and tapped her foot, trying to rechannel the anger she had before she opened the door, but his full lips and almond-shaped eyes were making it difficult for her to do anything but desire him.

"So, you gonna let me in, or are we gonna just stand in the cold?" One eyebrow hitched as he spoke to her.

"You can stand in the cold if you want to, but I'm gonna go back in and try to get some sleep like I was doing before your rude ass showed up at my door unannounced, ringing my bell, and knocking on it like the police with a search warrant for a criminal. Who do you think you are?"

"A man who needs to talk to you." He stepped into her space.

She could feel the heat of his breath warming her all over. She slowly licked her lips trying to provide moisture to her mouth.

He stared at her lips questioning if he should just devour her in a kiss, but his need to tell her just how he felt about her disappearing act overshadowed his hunger for her and he denied himself the taste of her lips.

Her chest heaving up and down as he heard the soft pants of her breath let him know that he had an effect on her. Good. It gave him the needed encouragement to say what he had come to say.

He inched closer to her still fighting the urge to kiss lips he knew were soft and supple as he stared at her with determination.

She took in a big gulp of air and refused to look at him but said, "I'm cold."

"Well let me in and close the door." He slowly rubbed his hands up and down her arms and could feel the goose bumps on them. He smiled inwardly believing he was the cause of them and not the brutal wind whipping past them and into the house.

"Get out of the way then." She was barely audible as she stared up at him. He towered her, but it wasn't his height that overwhelmed her, it was his presence. His essence.

He gently brushed past her and walked into her living room. He scanned his surroundings noting how dark it was in the room and that she had clothes strewn all over the place. It was a vast difference from the neat and kempt Kim he'd met months ago and had taken such an unfamiliar liking to. He took a seat on the couch she had vacated before she opened the door.

Kim remained in the foyer pacing her breathing. She thought she would have a few more days to gather herself before ending things with Darius. He had a certain charm about him that wooed her even though she'd never admit it to anyone, probably never to herself either. She breathed another deep sigh and made her way to the living room after closing the door behind her.

His scent hit her senses long before he came in sight and caused her to mumble to herself, "Okay, Kim. You can do this. Just tell him it's over, put him out, and get some sleep."

She crossed the threshold separating the foyer from the living room but didn't make her way back to where she once laid.

He had taken off his coat and she could see his biceps flexing under his fitted cardigan as he shifted on the couch upon her entry. His smooth skin had warmed over after being in the house and out of the brisk air outside. Any other time he was at her house, she would moan at the sight of his neatly trimmed, low beard that connected to his sideburns and goatee which aided in his sex appeal. She had never seen another man wear a low fade and waves the way he did. His lips looked so kissable even as he sat there warily staring at her.

It seemed as if the defiance he had festering in him when she opened the door had now been replaced with concern as he stared at her. Her thinning frame. Kim had worn slacks to work. Ones that he had peeled off of her well-defined thighs many times he stopped by one day after work. To see her pants so loose-fitting on her alarmed him. He didn't care if she was losing weight the right way through exercise and proper nutrition, but he could tell from the dark circles around her eyes that her makeup wasn't concealing and the fact that her normally big bright eyes were lackluster and sunken in, that something was off.

Kim was furious and yet endeared the more Darius stared at her. She could tell by the hint of surprise mixed with deep concern in his eyes that he was taken aback with her appearance. She needed to get rid of him soon before he started digging into more of her garden of secrets. She wasn't willing to share her issues with him, or anyone else for that matter.

"What are you looking at?"

"You," he said.

"I don't know why. There will be no sex tonight, buddy," Kim said as she took a seat on the couch across from him. She stared at him staring back at her. She wanted him, her body just didn't show signs of it. She hit the throw pillow next to her in frustration wishing the old her was alive. If so, she would pounce on him and experience the ride of her life she was sure to have as he worked his magic on her.

"I've told you before, we don't always have to have sex when we're together. In fact, that's why I came over here. What's up with you avoiding me and ignoring my calls?" He folded his hands and rested them on his lower stomach as he leaned back on the couch. He knew enough about Kim to keep an unassuming posture as he asked her questions. If she detected a fight in him, she would erect that brick wall of hers quick and hurl one sarcastic comment after another at him until he let her win whatever battle they were having at the moment.

"Since we're not in a relationship, I don't have to make myself available to you all of the time. I thought we understood that from the beginning." She folded her arms across her chest and stared directly at him.

"Yeah, but..."

"But what?" She demanded he continue his thought.

Darius let out a long sigh and rubbed his jet-black beard wondering if he was really ready to go there with Kim. They were being more serious than they ever had been. He sat up and rested his elbows on his knees and stared at her. "But don't you want more now?"

"No," Kim said flatly, hoping to mask the odd emotions swirling in her stomach. She didn't know if she honestly needed to throw up or if her heart and stomach were in cahoots with one another over his question.

"So you mean to tell me it's just sex between us? There's nothing else that's kept you coming back to me all of this time?" Darius perched his head on his interlaced hands and stared at Kim.

"Nothing more than sex. That's all it was."

"I'm not buying what you're trying to sell me. Before you pulled this disappearing act on me, I saw it in the way you looked at me. We don't just have sex, Kim, we make love. The way you lock your legs around me after we come together, as if you want us always to remain connected, one. What we have between us is more than just sex."

Kim couldn't handle herself under his stare. Her brain didn't want to agree with what he was saying but it seemed like her heart wasn't in tune with her thoughts. Even the way he described their time in bed sent tingles up and down her spine and her womanhood begin to awaken. *Maybe if I go take more B12 pills, we can do it one last time before I kick him out for good.* She stared off into the kitchen, refusing to lock eyes with him again. "You're wrong."

"Why can't you look me in my eyes and tell me I'm wrong then?"

Kim could tell by the thumping of her heart, the intensity of his cologne magnifying, and the soft tread of his boots hitting the floor that he had gotten off the couch and was walking towards her. He sat down beside her and grabbed her hand. He tugged on her arm a bit. "Kim, what's wrong?"

"Nothing." He was sexy, endearing, and annoying all at the same time. His caress on the back of her hand reminded her of how gentle he made love to her at times. The fact that he wasn't all over her trying to have sex and the tenderness in his voice let her know that he genuinely was concerned about her and for that, he annoyed her. It wasn't supposed to be that way with him.

He had already outlasted any other man she had casual yet exclusive sex with. And if she were honest with him, she'd tell him that he had been the best she ever had. The way he was so in tune with her body and needs as they had sex frightened her because she never wanted it to end with him. She had convinced herself that she could do without a relationship with him, but the sex, she craved that. Which is why she needed to hurry up and end things with him. For one, she needed to detox from him and her need of him inside of her. Two, clearly, he felt more for her than she did for him and it was turning into a problem she needed to avoid given her health issues. Which led into reason three, she was dying and wanted to do it alone.

He gently gripped her chin forcing her to face him. "Kim, don't kill me for saying this but you, you don't look your best."

She cocked her head to the side as one eyebrow lifted and she stared at him.

He reached up and rubbed her cheek. "I'm not trying to be rude. I'm just saying you aren't filling out your clothes the way you used to." He rubbed his hands up and down her thighs. "These used to be more muscular, thicker. And your eyes."

"What about my eyes?" Kim was on the brink of crying. Everyone had always raved about how beautiful her big eyes were, but she despised them now looking in the mirror at herself since her sickness returned.

If he thought she looked bad now she could only imagine the horrified look on his face if he saw her without the makeup on, or even worse, five months down the road. If she lasted that long. Nope, she wouldn't do that to him. Not only did his words let her know that he wanted more from her, but the way he sat there staring at her, caressing her. She reasoned after her first bout with cancer that being in a relationship was too risky, she knew life wasn't guaranteed. It made no sense to her for two people to love each other so that if one died the other felt like they would die, too. She thought no person should have to watch the love of their life slip away from them because of an illness. She couldn't risk love and she wouldn't risk Darius's heart.

"They're not as bright as they normally are. I remember back at Vance and Pam's wedding dinner you coughed a lot but told the group you had a bug. You've lost more weight since then and your face is starting to sink in. Baby, what's wrong?"

"Baby?" Kim was honestly shocked. "We don't use those kinds of terms with each other." She jumped up from the couch and away from him. He was too much for her. Exhaustion was overtaking her and not just from her sickness, but the gentle way he looked at her, talked to her. His presence was clouding her judgment to resist him. That overwhelmed her.

He got up from the couch and walked to her. She pulled back from him but he stepped closer to her until he had her pinned against the wall.

Too tired to put up a fight, she didn't move one bit.

"Well things have changed."

"What's changed, Darius?"

"My feelings for you."

Kim didn't like where the conversation was going so to end it, she wrapped her arms around his neck and pulled him into an all-consuming kiss. She moaned as she reacquainted herself with the taste of his tongue.

In turn, he fitted his body against hers as he lifted her off the ground and she instinctively wrapped her legs around his waist.

He was lost in her kiss when he remembered he hadn't said all that he wanted to say. He pried his lips away from her plump ones. "We're not done talking, Kim."

"Yes, we are." She leaned in and nibbled on that spot behind his ear she knew would drive him wild. She licked and bit him there before puckering kisses to the tender area.

"Damn." He let out a moan as she grinded on him.

"Take me to the bed now," she said against his skin.

"Damn." He knew he'd lost this battle with her as he rushed to her bedroom. He really did want to talk to her but he hadn't connected with her in so long that his manhood was painfully pressing against his jeans. *I'll give in to what we both want. But we're talking about an us before I leave.*

They made it to Kim's room and Darius laid her on the bed. *Maybe if I can't tell her how I feel, I'll show her.* He quickly discarded his clothes, but took his time in undressing her as he kissed her from head to toe, nipping at her inner thighs, relishing in the way she squirmed under him.

To avoid the pain, she suffered under his tender touch last time, every time he tried to fondle her breasts she locked hands with him.

"Please don't make me wait any longer."

The hoarseness in her voice drove him right inside of her and their bodies moved in sync with one another right until a powerful orgasm hit him causing him to collapse on her.

"Ouch," she screamed out in discomfort.

"What?" He lifted off her into a plank position as he looked into her scared eyes. "What's wrong?"

She pushed him off her and rolled onto her side so that her back faced him.

Confused, he stared at her before falling onto the bed beside her. He rested on his elbow as he observed her. To add to the list of things noticeably different about her, he took note of how her endurance wasn't what it used to be. But that wasn't what jarred him the most. He was baffled how she could turn her back on him after he had treasured her body the way he did. "I don't get it."

She didn't respond to him so he continued on. "I don't understand how together our bodies just created the best punch line to a joke I've ever wrote, heard, but now the air between us is like I just told you a corny knock-knock joke."

If it were any other time, Kim would call him out on the analogy he made of their sexual experience, but hey, he was a comedian. She guessed it was the best he could come up with to explain what just happened between them. It was a powerful moment between them. None like she'd ever experienced with him before, with any man for that matter. She felt his heart with every long stroke inside of her. She almost wanted to bare her soul to him, but his fall onto her tender breasts reminded her of what she was dealing with. The fate that lay ahead for her was dire. She couldn't explore something serious with him.

She tried to hold her tears back as long as she could. She was mad because she couldn't keep up with him in bed and even more mad at the empathy he showed her for not doing so. She saw the look in his eyes earlier when he first saw her. She knew she looked different to him, but he didn't call her out on it. For that she was grateful, and when he realized his stare was lingering on her appearance longer than it should have, he redirected his attention elsewhere.

Darius didn't know what was wrong with Kim, all he knew was the way her shoulder slightly heaved up and down was reminiscent of a person crying. He drew closer to her and pulled her snug against him as he wrapped his arms around her.

The way he cradled her body next to his, the gentle caresses his fingers traced circles on her arm, and the way he intermittently kissed her shoulder pained her. She realized her feelings for him were more than just sex, she cared about him in a way she had never done any other man.

She'd never felt a more tender embrace than the one consuming her at the moment. As the tears streamed her face, she thought back on the time spent with Darius over the past months. She thought she had did a god job of keeping her wall up and him at an arm's length, but his presence said otherwise.

The epiphany scared her and made her realize she had to get him out of her bed and out of her life.

11

It was Thursday afternoon, which Kim dreaded because it meant after work she'd have to go to chemo. She didn't even bother to drive to work that morning.

Since she'd promised Dr. Ngyuen she wouldn't drive herself home after the session, she didn't want to worry herself getting her car home and then to chemo in time for her appointment. She'd chosen Thursdays for her chemo days since her school often had half-days on Thursday. She didn't bother to go to work on Friday's. She merely called in knowing there would be a substitute readily available in the building or one could be quickly dispatched to the site. Either she was going to keep up a front at work or one with the sisterhood. She decided on the latter.

Taking Fridays off after her session would help her recoup possibly enough to hang out for a bit with the ladies since their weekends had become more active blending the new group of friends that Vance brought along.

The bell rang and she walked out with the kids and headed straight to her Uber.

She breathed a sigh of relief as she sat in the backseat grateful that she'd managed to escape Pam that day. She had a rough night the day before and knew she looked bad.

She didn't get much sleep after she kicked Darius out. The pained look on his face pierced her core and she missed his embrace as she laid in bed alone. The longer she stayed up restless, the more she realized that she wanted him, but keeping him in her life would be just too emotional for him and her.

Dr. Ngyuen had already informed her that she would be checked weekly for the progression or the recession of her cancer. She had the gut feeling that the tests that day wouldn't prove favorable for her. She'd made her bed a long time ago and she was definitely lying in it now.

***

Kim didn't pull away from Dr. Ngyuen as she gripped her hand, nor did she have a smart comeback for what she'd just heard.

"I'm sorry, Kim. You've only had one round of treatment so we just have to believe that it will work in the long run."

Kim sighed. She had been experiencing the pain in her breasts and had noted the ever-forming lumps. She knew they were cancer ridden well before it was confirmed. "Doc, I appreciate your positivity, but let's be real here." She turned and pointed to the wall illuminating her CT scans. "The X-ray on the right shows three times more masses than the one on the left." She pointed to her breasts. "These things are getting more and more cancerous."

"Well, we can wait out the chemo and radiation therapy or you can get them removed."

"I might've given that option serious thought if the cancer was centralized there, but as it shows," she pointed back to the illuminated wall displaying her full body scan x-rays, "I have cancer in pretty much my entire upper body. I might as well die with my boobs still attached."

"Kim, I have seen a lot of patients with similar diagnoses as yours and yet they came out strong and survived. I believe it was because of their hope and resilient spirit and will to live. You can't give up hope. You can't give up. You're not built for quitting."

Tears burned her eyes and streamed her face. "You say I'm not built for quitting, but I must be built for suffering. You've been here through every diagnosis. My body continues to be riddled with cancer. I've had to deal with one kind after another for over a decade. I'm tired, Doc. I have no more fight left in me." Kim finally pulled her hand from Dr. Ngyuen's grasp and covered her face in shame as she cried. She'd never let anyone see her that emotional.

"I suspect you're still trying to do this on your own. You still haven't told your family?"

Kim shook her head.

"Kim, draw on strength from your family. If they're anything like you, I know they have enough fight in them to help you get through this." She rubbed Kim's back.

"I can't tell them. I'm the strong one."

"Let them be your strength. We all need someone to lean on in times of crisis. And from what you've told me over the years about your family, I'm sure they are more than able to see you through this."

"I just can't." Kim wiped her face, squared her shoulders, and fled Dr. Ngyuen's office en route to her treatment session.

12

Vance and Pam were hosting everyone at their house that Friday night. With Monica and Pam now married, the sisterhood was spending even more time with each other. Their new get togethers included them bringing their spouses, but that didn't seem to bother them since the spouses blended into their friendship smoothly. However, the ladies arrived at Pam's house earlier than when they knew the rest of the guests would. They wanted to talk amongst themselves.

Pam had told Monica and Renee how different, grave, Kim looked at work when she last saw her. She shared with them how Kim had missed work earlier that day in addition to her taking an Uber home rather than drive her luxury SUV that she loved so much.

All three sat in Pam's comfy living room awaiting Kim's arrival as they chatted.

"You sure she'll show up tonight?" Monica looked to Renee.

"Well, when I called her earlier after Pam told me she wasn't at work again, she answered groggy after my fourth try saying that she would see me later and to stop calling and texting her before she hung up on me."

Monica shook her head with a hint of a grin on her face. "That sister of yours is something else."

"Seriously you all. What are we gonna do about her? She's denying the fact that she's pregnant and she's looking awful in the process."

"You really think Kim is pregnant?" Renee asked.

"To me it's the only thing that could explain her behavior," Monica said. "We all know her declaration of never getting married or having kids. Granted we don't know where and why it appeared because she didn't talk like that in high school. That happened after college. Maybe it really is keeping her from opening up to us about it. And if she's lost weight the way you say she has, the stress of it all has taken a toll on her."

"We know how Kim can be up in your business but hush about hers. Do you think she'll really tell us if she's pregnant? I mean just think about the times she's up and disappeared to foreign destinations for the entire summer or Christmas breaks. All we got were, 'Hey guys, I'm in Paris. See ya when I get back.' We accepted her impromptu trips over the years without inquiry, but in this case, she's gonna have to fess up to us," Pam said.

"Agreed," Renee consorted.

Just then, the doorbell rang.

Pam rushed to open it with Monica and Renee on her heels. Pam opened the door and they all fell silent as they stared at Kim.

"Keep looking at me like that and see don't I turn around and go right back home." Kim snipped at them.

They remained silent and stepped aside to let her enter. When they figured she was out of earshot, they whispered amongst themselves.

"Oh, sweetie. It's gonna be alright," she said, rubbing Renee's back as she cried.

"I have never seen my sister look so ghastly." She wiped more of her tears. "Honestly, I've always admired how beautiful she was, but that in there is not my sister. There's no sparkle in her eyes like normal. And Kim doesn't get skinny, she gets toned. What is wrong with her?" Renee muffled her mouth with her hand as she ran off to the bathroom.

"Honestly, she just looks tired...and yeah, she's lost some weight, but she's still beautiful," Monica said, taking a deep breath trying to make sense of the matter.

"Kim will always be beautiful, Mon, but you know just as well as I do that there's something big going on with her that's she's not telling us about."

Renee returned from the bathroom just as Pam and Monica were heading into the living room. She stopped as Monica raised her hand to speak to them. "Okay, we've all been the target of the group's interrogation when we were hiding something from the others. We each eventually caved in and helped one another to overcome the battle we were dealing with, but Kim has never been that target. We know she's different and won't respond to the same tactics used on us. We have to approach her differently," Monica said.

"Agreed," Pam said.

"Yup," Renee said, wringing her hands together.

"Okay, I know y'all out there talking about me. Come in here and say it to my face," Kim yelled as best as she could from the living room.

"Well, there's still some of that sass left in her," Monica said and chuckled as she led the pack into hopefully what hadn't transformed into the lion's den.

They headed in and sat in a configuration around the room that forced Kim to be the center of attention.

She ignored their stares at she gripped her knees into her chest and further snuggled under the throw blanket that was on the couch when she got there.

Monica spoke up first. "Kim, we could beat around the bush with you trying to get it out of you, but since that's not your style, maybe we should just get straight to the point." She looked to Pam and Renee for assurance, when they shrugged their shoulders she continued on. "What has the doctor said about the baby? Your weight loss?"

Kim stared at Monica. Her eyebrows slowly raised with a hint of merriment and yet bewilderment. "Why won't you dimwits listen to me when I say that I'm not pregnant? I just have this stomach virus that won't go away." Kim coughed. She was cold and weak. Chemo the day before was grueling to her system, but she knew continuing to stay away from the sisterhood would only further raise their suspicions and there was no telling what story they would come up with next trying to make sense of her weight loss and decaying facial features. No, she'd just have to face them head on and lie right to their faces that everything was alright with her. She'd try to get them to believe that she'd be back to herself in due time. Needing a blanket to keep her warm and always needing to lay down would just become the new staple for her whenever they hung out.

After staring back at Kim in wonder for so long, Renee walked over to the couch Kim was on. "Sissy, please tell us what exactly is wrong with you then." Renee lifted Kim's feet high enough to sit on the couch with her and lowered them onto her lap. She rubbed Kim's shin waiting on her to answer.

"I told you I have a stomach bug." Kim covered her mouth to stifle her fake cough to mask the tears welling up in her eyes. Although, they were being nosey, she loved her friends and her sister and Renee's touch sent her emotions haywire. She hadn't felt a loving touch since Darius's the other night. It really was a lot for her going through chemo alone, but again, she thought it was her punishment for having sex before marriage as a teenager. It was just her way of looking at her situation. Not that she thought God was punishing her but she took heed to the scripture that said if you sow of the flesh you shall reap corruption. That logic and the fact that she was counted on to be the fixer in the family and among her friends kept her tight-lipped about her diagnosis.

Just when they were huddling around her and she continued to cough, the doorbell rang.

"I'll get it," Vance called out from the kitchen where he'd been cooking.

"Excuse me, y'all," Pam said and left to join Vance to greet their guests.

Soon, Marcus and his wife, Tameka; Anthony and his wife, Brandy; Andrew, and Darius appeared. Everyone filed into the living room ready to get game night underway except for Darius.

He saw Kim's SUV outside and knew she had to be there as well. He wished he wasn't anxious to see her, but being honest with himself, he missed her something awful and couldn't wait to lay his eyes on her, but when he did, his heart dropped. And not in the soul-stirring happy way he normally was to see her, but he was worried and nervous as to why she kept looking more fragile each time he saw her. She looked drain. *What is making her like this?* He wanted to rush to her side to get answers from her. Like why she kicked him out the other night and why she's back to avoiding him. But because he'd never felt so strongly, so attracted to a woman as he did Kim, he felt he needed to play it safe, keep it cool. *Hell, maybe this thing I have for her will wear off.* He looked at her pale face almost covered with the blanket over it. *Oh, who I am kidding, I won't be getting over her anytime soon. Damn! Why won't she let me in?* His inner battle of feelings for Kim raged on as he decided to remain cool and keep his distance from her in the room.

"Hi, Kim. You okay?" Marcus's wife, Tameka, asked as she stood near Kim.

"Yeah, I'm okay. Just a little under the weather."

Darius leaned against the wall across the room with his arms folded across his chest. He avoided looking in Kim's direction, but he craned his neck and strained his ears trying to catch every word said to her and her responses.

"Well I hope you feel better soon," Tameka said.

"Me, too." Anthony's wife, Brandy, chimed in.

"I'll be praying for your rapid healing," Marcus said to Kim as he took a seat by his wife.

"Thanks." Kim barely got her words out before she went into a coughing fit.

Darius lifted himself off the wall ready to get to Kim but remembered he was supposed to be playing it cool. Instead of heading straight towards her, he went and sat on a high stool near the fireplace.

Renee, however, rushed to Kim's side. "Sissy, are you okay? That cough doesn't sound good."

Kim's cough finally subsided. She spoke through a strained voice. "I'm okay. I just need some water."

With that admission, Monica jumped from the floor near Kim's feet and rushed to the kitchen to get a bottled water. She returned with it and gave it to Kim. The sisterhood huddled over her as she drank.

She knew they were all looking at her as they stood over her still wrapped tightly in the blanket, which was uncommon for her. She was normally always hot. "Girls, simmer down and go sit with your men." She snarled at them as a smile crept on her face.

Monica pointed her finger at Kim. "This is not over. We'll finish our discussion later."

"Don't bet on it." Kim took another swig of the water and closed the top on it before pulling the cover pretty much over her nose.

With that view of her face, and when she wasn't looking in his direction, Darius found himself staring at big eyes that once held so much valor and sparkle but seemed to be dimming and sinking in more and more each time he saw her. He was snapped out of his trance as Renee refuted Kim's last statement.

"Go to our men? Everyone is not a couple here." Renee definitely had become more vocal since she had lifted the burden of her secret of not having an abortion in college but rather giving the baby up for an adoption.

Andrew's eyebrow hitched and he cleared his throat as he stared at Renee which sent the room in an uproar of laughter.

Renee walked over to her seat which just happened to be right next to Andrew on one of the loveseats in the spacious yet cozy sunken living room.

"So, you don't have a man? We aren't a couple?" Andrew asked Renee.

She giggled as she stared at him. "Stop being silly. You know we agreed that I still need to figure out what I'll do about my son and you about your father, Charles, before we take *us* any further."

The heated stare Andrew set on Renee caused her to fall into that familiar habit of playing with the hem of her shirt as she averted eye contact with him.

"Well, I don't want to wait anymore." He leaned over until he was in front of her. He stared into her eyes, seeing both hesitation and admiration for him. The latter shined brighter and gave him the clearance he needed. He leaned in and his lips crashed into hers.

She raised her hands in a weak objection but he interlocked his hand with hers and deepened their kiss. She cooed as he explored her mouth and he smiled against her lips knowing he wouldn't get any further objections from her. When he hesitantly pulled back from her they stared into each other's eyes. Andrew broke the silence in the room first. "So we still aren't a couple?"

Renee's eyebrows raised in merriment as she bit the corner of her bottom lip and tightened her grip on his hand. "We are."

"Finally," Kim said as she adjusted in her space to rest on her other side.

Renee smiled as she looked at Kim. "You'll have a finally soon, too." She thought about how the baby would hopefully bring Darius and Kim closer, marriage hopefully.

"Again, don't bet on that..." Kim's words trailed off as she finally locked eyes with Darius for the first time that night. The look in his eyes shifted from a tinge of hurt in response to what she said and then shifted to a determined 'I'll prove you wrong' look. The longer they stared at one another the more intense his look became until Kim had no choice but to look away.

She coughed as her body heated up. She threw the covers off her and grabbed her water hoping it would cool her off. Darius's presence and stare was doing an unusual attack on her nerves.

Everyone stared at her.

"You okay?" Keith said.

She finished sipping her water before she shot a 'mind your business' look at him. "Yeah, can't a girl have a hot flash?"

"I guess," Keith said to Kim before turning his attention back to Andrew and his other sister, Renee. His nostrils flared and he folded his bulging arms across his firm chest as he tapped his foot. He continued staring at them with their hands interlaced and Renee resting her head on Andrew's shoulder.

She finally sat up. "What?"

"I don't think he has an issue with you, he has one with me. Look, Keith, everyone in this room should be able to tell how much I care about Renee. How she's helped me grow as a man. I don't wanna wait any longer to start something serious with her." Andrew's deep voice seemed to plead with Keith for permission to date his sister.

Renee squeezed his hand pulling him back from getting up from the couch. "You or I don't have to explain anything to Keith."

"Oh really?" Keith's eyebrows raised in challenge as his six foot two frame stood and inched over to the couch where Andrew and Renee sat.

The rest of the room was silent as Monica tried pulling him back. "Keith, sit down."

He ignored his wife's request and kept moving forward until he towered over Andrew.

Renee shot up out of her seat. "Yes, really. The way you and Monica are always around us smooching and carrying on, you can't tell me and my grown man what we can and can't do." Renee's hand was still locked with Andrew's and she pulled him up from the couch to stand beside her.

Keith continued to breathe heavy with his nostrils flared as he practically stood nose to nose with Andrew. "Is that right, Andrew?"

"Yeah, man." Andrew's voice seemed to drop an octave lower than how deep it normally was. "Yeah, man. I'll fight you for her if I have too." His jaws tightened.

Monica had now come to Keith's side and tugged on his arm. "Keith, go sit back down and leave them alone. Renee is right."

He stared a little longer at Andrew before he buckled over in laughter.

The women's faces remained contorted in confusion, but soon all the men, except Andrew joined Keith in laughing.

Keith stood up still chuckling. He gripped his stomach trying to quell his laughter. "My man." He extended his hand to shake Andrew's and when Andrew accepted, he pulled him in for a brotherly embrace, patting him on the back as he continued laughing.

"What? So, you weren't serious? You were just joking with him?" Renee, with her shoulders hunched and her eyebrows furrowed, asked still confused.

Her facial expression, body language, and tone of voice sent the entire room in an uproar of laughter. They clung to each other and a few wiped their eyes of tears as they tried to settle themselves.

Renee, annoyed by them laughing at her, hit both Keith and Andrew on their arms. She hit Keith harder though before turning her attention to Andrew first. "So, you knew he was joking?"

"No." Andrew finally stopped laughing. "But I can understand the way he was acting, and looking back, it's funny." He chuckled again, but stifled it immediately seeing the hurt look on Renee's face. He put his arm around her waist but she shooed him away. Her cute pout made him work hard to continue to contain his laughter.

Renee pointed at Keith. "And you, you jerk—"

Keith cut her off as he pulled her into a hug. "You'll get over it. I was only joking. Besides, I didn't get a chance to do the big brother act with that jerk, Ted, you dated in college. I had to do it in life at least once. Since I have a feeling that Andrew's the one for you, I had to put the show on now." Keith planted a kiss on her cheek, but she quickly wiped it off as she pulled back from his face, but not out of his embrace as he wouldn't let her.

"You're still a jerk."

"I'll take that." He smiled.

Keith's smile reminded her so much of her son that she quickly dismissed her anger at him and kissed him on his cheek. "I love you, too."

Renee and Keith finally broke apart and he whispered in Monica's ear as they headed back to their seats.

Renee turned to Andrew with a wary stare as he stood next to her with his lips puckered up. "Where's my kiss?"

"Oh whatever." She found herself finally laughing at the situation as she pulled Andrew down on the couch with her. As conversations around the room got underway, she leaned in and gave him a sweet kiss on his cheek, but he wasn't satisfied with that. He cupped her chin and pulled her in for another passionate kiss not wanting to pull away until Kim's constant fake clearing of her throat pulled their lips apart from one another.

"Okay, clearly you two are officially a couple, but this is game night, so let's get this show on the road. Sleep will be calling me soon and I must answer it." Kim, cold again, pulled the cover tighter around her body and rested her head on her knees.

"Scrooge, we'll let the night flow as it should," Pam said as she braced herself on Vance's knee to stand from where she sat on the couch. She headed to a table behind one of the couches and grabbed one of the many games littering it. "Taboo anyone?"

Kim scanned the sunken living room. Vance's décor was nice, but so was Pam's condo that she had custom designed just a year ago. A question brewed in her. She wasn't one to mince words, so she didn't feel the need to delay in asking her question until she had Pam alone. It didn't matter to her that everyone else was focused on what game to play. "Um, I don't care what game y'all play," She looked over at Pam. "I wanna know why you moved here to Vance's house instead of staying in that beautiful condo you personally designed just last year? Why do women always have to give up stuff when they say I do?" Kim asked the latter question thinking about how much of her future she would be forfeiting to her sickness. She didn't want her best friend to lose her identity, let alone to a man.

"Vance, don't mind her." Pam looked at him.

"I don't. You forgot I've worked with her a long time. I know how upfront she can be." He laughed and took a swig of his coke.

"Good, because I liked you as my boss but now I have to love you as my best friend's husband. So, no need to take offense to me, just go with the flow." Kim started laughing but soon got choked up. She grabbed her water bottle but it was empty. She got up to get some more water but Renee stopped her in her tracks.

"I'll get it for you, sissy."

"I'm not an invalid. I can get it myself," Kim sniped and coughed as she made her way up the few stairs and into the foyer area in search of the kitchen.

"But you don't even know where the kitchen is," Renee said.

"I have eyes, don't I? They'll help me find it eventually." Kim gripped the throw blanket tighter around her.

"Scrooge," Renee called out after Kim.

"Let the games begin," Pam said, commencing game night.

"I'll show you where it is." Darius' deep voice warmed Kim's core as he came up behind her.

"I can find it just fine on my own." Kim refused to look back at him and walked forward as fast as she could. She turned her head from side to side in search of what she soon found right ahead of her.

"You are so stubborn, woman," Darius said as he followed behind her.

"See, I found it on my own just fine. You can go back in there with them."

Kim walked into the spacious, warm, open concept kitchen full of earth tone rich colors. It actually mirrored Pam's condo with the skylight and all, just bigger. She could see why Pam chose to move in with him.

She opened the stainless steel double door refrigerator and spotted the bottled water, but almost threw up from the mix of smells emanating from the refrigerator and what Vance had brewed on the stove.

She cupped her mouth as she jerked forward trying to keep the little of nothing she had in her stomach in it.

Darius put aside his pride and rushed to her side. "Kim, you okay?" He gently gripped her arm as she stood up again.

"Yeah. I'm okay." She pulled away and stepped back from him. Coming to her rescue again with such compassion in his voice confused her. Her heart seemed as if it wanted to bask in his adoration of her, but her head, her good common sense, knew she needed to stay clear of him. "Darius, I'm fine. Now will you let me drink my water in peace?"

"Kim, what changed between us?" No one could misunderstand the confused tone in his voice. He stepped back from her and rubbed his neck in angst.

She swallowed her water and squared her shoulders as best as she could as she looked him straight in the eyes. "You changed, Darius. You changed. We wanted the same thing in the beginning, but now you want more than what we do. I don't."

He moved close to her and towered over her as he reached down and touched her face, willing his finger and palm to gently caress her cheek.

She closed her eyes and took in the moment. His ocean breeze smell. His warm, gentle strokes across her face. The heat and strength of his body against her. Why couldn't she have met him before her first diagnosis? Maybe she could've given her heart to him then, but not now. She kept her eyes closed as the tears stung them.

Seeing her taking in his touch, he spoke hoping to seal the deal with her. "Kim, let's just give us a try." He lowered his head until his mouth was mere inches from hers. He could feel the heat of her breaths on his skin which made him place his other hand on the small of her back and pulled her in for a kiss.

At first, their lips just melded together in peace, but he wanted more. He ran his tongue along the seam of her lips and when he heard the soft whimper escape her lips, he forged his tongue into her mouth exploring it with a thirst he didn't want quenched. He held on tighter to her as he felt her body relax against him. He continued to caress her face as his passionate kiss told her just how much he cared for her.

She moaned and gripped his neck as her knees buckled.

He trailed kisses down her neck and her head fell back, accepting what he was offering her.

"Be mine please," he mumbled against her neck.

And just like that, his request snapped her out of the trance he had her in for the last few but passionate minutes.

Her eyes fluttered before finally staying open. She pushed him off her and took in a deep breath trying to gather her wits. His full lips and kisses had become so much more potent in their last few encounters than ever before.

The lights in the kitchen were dim but she clearly saw the confused look on his face as his eyebrows furrowed together and his arms stretched upward in a questioning motion. "What?"

She wiped her mouth with the sleeve of her shirt as if trying to rub off for good the effect he had on her. "Darius, no." She injected venom in her voice and shot him a manufactured look of disgust. We will never be what you want us to be." She rushed from the kitchen to the bathroom, leaving Darius dazed.

She made it to what had become her sanctuary since she started chemo and heaved every little bit of food she had consumed that day. She leaned over the toilet with her hands on her thighs crying. She didn't know she relieved herself because of the after effects of chemo that week or because of the disheartening look of hurt in Darius eyes when she told him they would never be what he wanted them to be.

Tears clouded her vision as she fell back against the wall sobbing silently. She couldn't afford for the sisterhood to hear her cries. It would really alarm them. She hated what had become of her life.

13

The crowd stared at Darius as he told one bad joke after another. The way Kim had left him last night had him in a funk the rest of the Friday night and all of Saturday morning.

He waited outside the bathroom door Kim ran into pleading for her to talk to him, but after twenty minutes of silence from her, he grabbed his jacket and headed back into the group of rowdy Taboo players and wished them a good night.

He ditched the fellas that Saturday morning for their routine pickup game and found himself laying around his condo all day moping, right up to the time he had to leave for the comedy club. He really didn't want to go but after texting back and forth with the owner, Miles, he knew he had to keep his commitment to the club. Besides, comedy was supposed to be his outlet, but looking out into the crowd via the dim lighting, the marred faces let him know his outlet wasn't working for him or for them.

Kim. He was already stumped coming into the club, but to see her finally sitting around the table with his friends after missing so many Saturday nights of his set, yet she refused to make eye contact with him, pained him and made his blood boil. How could she grab a hold of his heart the way she did but not accept it? The answer to that question stumped him more than any he'd ever asked before.

"Give it up for Darius the Louse, ladies and gentleman," Miles said, coming on the stage as he patted Darius on the back but snatched the mic out of his hands. "Now if you're a regular here, you know the man really is funny. He must've just left that particular bone out of his body tonight. We'll give that dog a second to go find his bone." Miles made a shooeing motion for Darius to leave the stage as he tried to pump the crowd back up.

Darius jumped off the low stage and bypassed his friends at the table and headed straight to the bar.

Of course, all of his friends, including Andrew, got up from their seats and followed him to the bar, leaving the women alone to talk amongst themselves. However, Keith remained at the table but checked his social media as the women spoke to one another.

"So, this is why y'all insisted I come out tonight? To listen to his bad jokes?" Kim said, shivering as she wrapped her knitted cardigan tighter around her body.

"I can't believe you're cold. It's hot in here," Monica said as she took her denim jacket off with nothing left but a burnout T-shirt on.

"Whatever, you know he's funny. Maybe it's your presence that messed him up for a second. It seemed like y'all ended on a sour note last night," Pam said, swirling her straw in her virgin daiquiri.

And as for Renee, she just stared at Andrew, marveling in the fact they were officially a couple.

"The man wasn't funny tonight. He was a louse, just like the owner called him."

"What's going on between you two?" Monica leaned in to be heard over the music that was now playing.

"Yeah, the way you been avoiding eye contact with him tonight and then he's either ogling you or looking at you with contempt. Was the argument that bad last night?" Pam chimed in.

"How many times must I tell you all that there was only sex between us? He wants more, I don't, so I cut him off for good last night."

"But what about the baby?" Renee asked.

"Baby?" Keith said loudly with a raised eyebrow as he stared at Kim.

She pursed her lips. "Keith, ignore them. I swear I'm not pregnant."

He looked her up and down, focusing on her stomach and then stared at her a bit longer before he said, "I guess I'll believe you for now." He slowly turned his focus back to his phone, but his ears were still in tune with the ladies conversation.

"Yeah, the baby. And from the looks he's giving you, things are far from over between you two," Monica said as she watched the mixed emotions on Darius's face as he deliberately stared at Kim.

Kim never turned to face him.

***

Darius leaned his lower back against the polished mahogany bar with his arms folded across his chest as he stared at Kim ignoring him.

"Well damn, man. Why don't you just go over there and say something to her? Staring at her the way you are, people might think you're a creep or something," Anthony said.

Darius looked to the right of him at Anthony and cut him a deathly glare before he turned his focus back on Kim.

"Darius, man, just say something to her. Shoot, say something to us. Is it like we thought it was? Do you really have it bad for her?" Marcus asked as he ushered the bartender away yet again. This time, Darius didn't go to the bar with the intent of drinking his thoughts of Kim away. He just went there to put some distance between him and her for the time being. But the soft jazz the band was playing wasn't helping his mood at all.

He and Kim were both fans of jazz and it was a mid-tempo song he and Kim had made love to one night. If he thought back, it might've been the first time it hit him that they made love rather than just had sex.

"Damn." He turned and pounded his fist on the bar, causing the contents of the patron's shot glass next to him to spill over. "Sorry, man." Darius looked at the man before beckoning the bartender, Chip, over. "Replace whatever he's drinking."

"Sure thing." Chip readied the drink and the patron tipped his head at Darius before returning his attention to his companion.

Darius finally rested on the stool near him and let his head drop onto his balled fists.

"D, man, you're losing your cool because you won't just man up and lay your cards on the table with Kim. You never know, she may want what you want," Vance said as he shrugged his broad shoulders.

"I have, but she ain't trying to hear it." Darius chuckled as he ran his hand over the waves in his head. "Her running away from me makes me wonder for a second if we're really meant to be."

"What?" Anthony said.

"I mean, do I like her a lot? Yeah? But love? I don't know if that's the case." He felt a twinge in his chest. He was lying to his guys, to himself. "Why I gotta chase someone who ain't trying to be caught?"

"Come on, man. You know women." Andrew finally joined in feeling comfortable with the men to add his thoughts. "They wanna know you see the value in them, so your pursuit of her just might seal the deal with her. Kim don't seem like the type that will give in to you after one romantic date."

The guys all laughed but it mixed in with the rest of the crowd as the owner told a joke before introducing the band for the night. The sounds of horns, bass guitars, and drums filled the air.

"This just ain't me. Wanting to be a one-woman man? Nah, I just must be butt hurt because she ain't giving in to me the way I want her to."

"Let me ask you this?" Marcus put his hand on Darius' shoulder. "Do you think about her first thing in the morning?"

The corners of Darius' full lips slightly curved up as he turned to face the table where Kim sat and settled his stare on her again.

"I'll take that as a yes. Do you think about her all throughout the day?"

The subtle curve in Darius' mouth drew higher up.

"And I'm not just talking about thinking about the last time y'all had sex. Which you know I don't agree with since y'all ain't married."

Darius smirked, pulling away from Marcus. "Man, I don't care what you do and don't agree with. And of course, I'm gonna think about what we do in bed. That woman is magnificent in bed." A sinister smile decorated Darius' face.

"Magnificent?" Anthony's eyebrow hitched high on his forehead.

"Yes, magnificent, magical." Darius laughed. "I ain't never been with another like her. Not sure if I want there to be another, either." He mumbled the last of his statement as a somber look donned his face and his shoulders slumped. He stared at Kim, refusing to look at him although she was sitting at an angle at the table that gave her just as much of a clear view of him as he had of her. He knew she was avoiding eye contact with him on purpose.

"I heard what you said," Marcus spoke up again. "Like I helped Vance to see that Pam was the one for him, I guess I gotta do that for you where Kim is concerned." Marcus shook his head.

"Man whatever." Darius playfully shoved Marcus in his shoulder.

"Seriously, marriage is a good and honorable thing." Marcus' tone was jolly yet serious.

Darius shot him an incredulous look. "Marriage? Ain't nobody said nothing about marriage. Marriage ain't even on the radar."

"Let me ask you this, have you talked to or had sex with anyone else since you been 'seeing' Kim?" Vance motioned his hands in air quotes mid-sentence.

"No."

"And why not?"

"I don't know, I just didn't get around to seeing someone else yet."

"Save that whack excuse for someone else. You're an Al B. Sure look-a-like. You get attention from ladies all the time. Especially from the one at the end of the bar."

Darius looked over to see Sam wink at him.

He let out a loud sigh as he snarled and directed his attention back to the fellas.

"I know you light skinned dudes have made a slight comeback, but us chocolate brothas are definitely still in the lead." Vance chuckled.

"Man, whatever. I don't look like Al B. Sure. All light skinned people don't look alike." Darius nudged Vance with his elbow.

"Seriously though, you haven't seen another woman since you've been 'seeing' Kim, which has been a little over a year, right?" Marcus asked.

"Yeah." Darius shook his head with reminded awareness of how long he'd been with Kim. "But that doesn't matter. It's not like we go out on dates all the time and we sit up sharing our pasts with one another. There's a lot that I don't know about that woman."

"Yeah, but it's what you do know about her that has you hooked on her. And naw, I ain't just talking about sex either." Vance held his hand up to silence a sermon from his brother Marcus. "I just got back right with God almost two years ago, but y'all know how I was before then."

"Yeah, a straight up ladies' man," Darius responded.

"Exactly. Truth be told, I had good and okay sex with some amazing women, but now I have amazing sex with Pam. And you wanna know why?" Vance poked Darius in the chest.

"Why Nietzsche, the great philosopher?" Darius asked, trying to keep a straight face.

"I'll be Nietzsche if that's what it takes to get through to your knucklehead. Man, Pam is my wife, our souls are intertwined. We connect on a whole other level. While I'm glad we did it God's way and waited until we got married before we had sex, I bet if we would've had sex when we first hooked up, it still would've been as explosive as it is now. You only experience that with the one that's truly for you."

"I agree with Vance. Especially about waiting until after marriage to have sex," Marcus chimed in. "And truth is, it's not about the quantity of time you spend with a person, it's about the quality of time you spend with them. So what if y'all haven't had many, if any, one on one dates. We've all been around each other a lot the past year and I see how y'all interact together. I've been told and can see how feisty she is but that doesn't always come across with you. You do know a lot about her, man. Think about all the Friday game nights we've had together. The conversations that came before and after the games. Kim was the main one speaking up and sharing her views on issues. You were the other loud mouth in the room."

The guys laughed, smirked, and chuckled at Marcus' jest.

"Seriously though, we all learn a lot about and from one another every time we meet. A person can act one way when you're alone, but it's how they act when others are around that gives you a great indication of who they are. So what if you haven't had candlelight dinners with her. You know her and you know you want her."

"Well preach then, bishop," Vance interjected, laughing but quickly leaned out of Marcus' reach to avoid the blow he was trying to deal him.

"Shut up, man." Marcus smirked at Vance but immediately turned his attention back to Darius. "I see how she looks at you and more importantly, I see how you look at her." Marcus tapped Darius' chest with two fingers before continuing to speak, "I'm telling you man, she's the one for you."

Darius breathed a deep sigh. It seemed as if Marcus had put the last nail in the coffin that would bury his old love life. He really did want Kim. He just needed to convince her of the same.

He grabbed the first unattended shot glass near him, gulped its contents down, slapped his chest trying to suffuse the sting it subjected him to, and then marched over to the table Kim sat at.

"Kim, I need to talk to you now," he said, standing next to her.

"We have nothing to talk about." She drew her cardigan closer around her and stared at the shiny brass saxophone doing its job on stage.

"Yes, we do." He grabbed her hand and his touch altered her breathing.

Monica leaned into Kim. "Will you just go with the man? Y'all are making a scene. Besides this is one of Keith and I's favorite songs and you all are interrupting it." Monica turned her attention back to the jazz band on stage as she snuggled close to Keith.

Kim mumbled an expletive under her breath at Monica. She saw the corner of Monica's mouth curve up indicating she had heard her.

Kim snarled as she finally looked up at Darius. "Okay, I'll go talk with you, but make it short." She grabbed her clutch purse and was getting out her seat when he pulled it back to assist her. She looked over her shoulder at him. "I can stand up just fine on my own."

He shook his head. *Lord help me get through to this stubborn woman.* He hoped his silent prayer would reach God's ears before they made it to the back of the club to talk.

When Darius finally cornered Kim at the back of the club, he grabbed her by her hand and held onto it tightly as she tried to pull away from him. The caresses his thumb rendered the back of her hand made it difficult for her to continue to resist him. She tried to free herself of his grip but gave up after realizing he just wouldn't let her go.

He rubbed his face in frustration and leaned down so that she could hear him and he could make eye contact with her. "Kim, look at me. Kim?" His voice softened as his stare intensified.

She could feel his eyes searing a hole through the side of her face. His calming ocean breeze scent inebriated her. The heat of his breath pulsing on her face made her close her eyes trying to draw strength from God only knows where before she forced herself to finally look at him.

Smoke machines had created a haze in the club and the lights were dim. He had her planted in an even darker corner. She was grateful for it because maybe, just maybe, the lack of light shining on them helped to hide the tremors he caused to her body. Again, she didn't know if it was her waning immune system wreaking havoc on her nerves or his presence.

Whichever one it was, the feeling of being out of control of her body was foreign to her and she needed freedom from it ASAP. "Darius," she said in the calmest tone she could as her eyes locked with his.

It took everything in him not to snatch her up in his arms and plant smoldering kisses all over her, but he had to try and get his point across to her yet again.

Her hand was more frail than it had been the last time he made love to her, so he lessened his grip on it but continued caressing the back of it.

"Kim." His voice was low, but the tone of his voice was intent. "Let's stop playing games. It's clear to everyone but you that we should be together."

She held her breath trying to slow down the rapid beats of her hearts. She knew what she should say, but she was too afraid what would come out and how it would sound if she did say something. She tried to turn her head away from him again but the gentle strokes of his hand tethering her cheek kept her eyes locked on him.

"Kim, I love you." The admission shocked Darius as he whispered the words, but realizing they were true, he leaned in close to her and cleared his throat before speaking again in confidence. "Kim, I love you."

Kim found herself lost in his eyes. She felt his love for her oozing from every pore of his body. From his ragged breathing to his squared shoulders, to the gentleness in his eyes. Tears welled in her eyes and she inwardly cursed her heart for betraying her. It was telling her that she did love him. Thoughts of a life with Darius had plagued her since the last time they made love. She had given up on having real love with a man and a family of her own with her first scare with cancer. However, Darius made her want him as her husband, the father of her children but just that awful feeling in the pit of her rotting stomach that her dance with cancer would end with the curtains closing for good this time.

She didn't think she would get an encore at life after this performance with cancer. She knew she cared enough about him to not put him through the pain of losing her. She needed to shake herself free of Darius for good. She hoped he'd get the picture she began to paint as she invoked stares of hate and disgust at him. "I hope you believe me when I say this. Leave me the hell alone. I don't love you and I never will." She snatched her hand from his and fled the club willing her tears to remain dormant until she made it home.

Darius kicked the wall before storming off to the bathroom.

***

Sam sat at the bar smirking having been privy to bits and pieces of the interaction between Kim and Darius. She smiled as she tilted her head back and swallowed the last of her mojito. She was excited that Kim left the way she did, but the way Darius stormed off gave her pause. Maybe he really was in love with Kim, and if so that definitely put a monkey wrench in her plans. But she would be unyielding in her pursuit. Darius would be hers, not Kim's.

14

"Congratulations on the baby, girl," Sam said, holding the cute little brown teddy bear out to her best friend as she made it to her bedside.

"Thanks." Myra smiled, looking at her six-hour-old daughter.

"Aw, she's so adorable." Sam patted the baby's curly afro. "My daughter's hair was just like this. Good luck with it when it's time to start combing it."

"I have a while before that happens, I'm just gonna enjoy her as she is." Myra bent down and rubbed her nose against the baby's.

"So, how are you?" Sam plopped down in the seat at the foot of the hospital bed and draped her oversized purse over her lap.

"Well, considering I just had a baby without an epidural."

Sam's eyes widened. "No, you didn't."

"Yes, I did. It was no choice of my own, though. I felt the pressure below, and thinking it would be like how it was when I had my boys, I took my time getting here. Big mistake. By the time I got here, the contractions had intensified quickly, and then my water broke. I was ready to deliver. I begged them for meds, but it was too late. That's okay, she was out with one push." Myra smiled as the baby stirred in her arms.

"So, are you happy now? You have your little girl after three boys."

"Yes, I am." Myra looked skeptically at Sam as her focus shifted to her from the baby. "And what about you, still trying to have a boy with Darius?"

"Don't start with me, Myra." Sam rose from her seat ready to leave the room if the conversation led to where it normally did whenever Darius was mentioned.

"Come on, Sam. I'm your best and one of your oldest friends. I'm supposed to keep it real with you."

"Keeping it real is one thing, but trying to run my life is a whole other thing."

"I'm not trying to run your life. I just hate to see how you are after it doesn't work with you chasing these men that don't want you."

Sam flopped back down in the seat. Her legs flew up before they finally rested on the floor again. Sam knew a recap of her sordid love life was next.

"All I'm saying is, you haven't been right with men since Brian. He played house with you before you were pregnant, but when it came time for him to step up to the plate as a father he hightailed it out of your life quicker than it takes to make instant oatmeal."

"Myra, I know what happened between Brian and me. I was there." Sam huffed and rolled her eyes.

"Well you must have forgot what it was like for you, for all of us, taking turns helping babysit Brianna while you worked and finished your undergrad degree in nursing. And even after that."

Sam stared out the window at her car in the parking lot. Myra's room overlooked the entrance of the hospital.

"You can tune me out if you want to, but Brian clearly was never into you the way you were into him if he could dismiss you and Brianna so easily. And you've managed to like that same kind of man repeatedly over the years. Now you're doing that same thing with Darius, going after a man that clearly doesn't want you."

"That's not true." Sam jumped out of her seat again with a sour face, staring at Myra.

"It's not? Brian didn't lead you on with talks of marrying you?" Myra switched her baby to rest in her other arm. "So how do you explain him abandoning you and Brianna only to start a life with that chick down in Houston?"

"I can't." Sam folded her arms across her chest, pouting, but summoned the rebellion to snap back at Myra. "Just because you found love with a great man your first time out the gate doesn't mean you know everything, Myra," Sam said with a slow eye roll.

"I didn't say I did, Sam. But what I do know is that men aren't as complex as we are. They see something they want, they go after it." Myra shook her head at Sam as she stood near the window pretending to ignore her.

"How long were you two fooling around?"

"For five months." Sam smiled finally looking at Myra. "And it was more than just fooling around," Sam mumbled.

Myra's eyebrow hitched knowing she would have to share the same precautionary lesson she shared with the attendees of the singles women's ministry meetings held weekly at her church. She kissed her baby's forehead before reluctantly placing her in the baby bed next to hers. She sat up more and folded her hands in her lap as she looked at Sam. "Did you ever meet his parents? His friends? Go to any work-related events with him? Attend church with him?"

In response to Myra's questions, Sam mumbled, "No, no, no, no."

"Well those are great indicators of whether or not he really wanted you in his life."

Sam turned to Myra with her nose turned up. "Again, I wanted to take things slow with him, so meeting those people or going those places with him didn't matter much to me." Sam turned her face to hide the frown marring it. She was lying and she knew Myra would be able to detect it, too.

Myra chose to ignore the fact that Sam was lying to her face and continue on. She had a newborn baby she wanted to get back to and a husband returning to the hospital soon but she wouldn't stop trying to get through to her best friend's thick skull. "Since you know we keep it real with one another,

I'll just stick to that method. Darius will never want you the way you want him, sweetie."

"I'm leaving." Sam shot Myra an annoyed stare and started towards the door, but the song Myra started singing kept her planted in the room.

"Always sisters, always friends, let's stay real close 'til the end, forgiving each other, letting love cover, always sisters, always friends," Myra sang joyously.

Myra, Sam, and their other best friend, Trice, agreed that after hearing the beautiful ode to friendships sang by CeCe Winans that if things ever got too heated between either of them one would sing the song as a reminder of their friendship and that they really did have each other's best interest at heart.

Sam pivoted on her heels and looked at Myra. "You know I'm only still here because I love to hear you sing. Now if that was Trice who belted that out, I would've ran faster than you can hit that button for a nurse."

They both laughed.

"Leave Trice alone. She's not here to defend her non-singing self. But really, Sam, just have a seat for a second and hear me out."

Sam huffed and hesitantly made her way back to the chair at the end of the bed.

"You know just as well as I do that giving it up to a man won't make him stay with you."

Sam rolled her eyes again.

"No matter how good you think your stuff is," Myra said in contest to Sam's defiant posture.

Sam pursed her lips at Myra.

"It's been how long since y'all last slept together?"

Sam paused dreading to say out loud just how long it'd been since she'd been intimate with Darius. "Over a year and a half," she muttered.

Myra was honestly shocked by the admission which was evident in her wide eyes and the way her mouth dropped open before she finally decided to speak. "Sam, the way you carry on about him, I would've thought you were just with him last night."

"You don't understand. You'll never understand."

"Yes, I do. You have a serious soul tie with him."

"A what?" Sam had grown up in church just like Myra, however, she hadn't stayed connected to God as she'd gotten older like Myra had. It was evident in the term Myra was slinging her way.

"A soul tie. When you're intimate, have sex with a person, the two of you form a mighty bond, a soul tie. That's why God cautions us against having sex before marriage. We should only be connected to our husbands or wives like that, but when we do things our way, we end up forming bonds with people that we shouldn't. And that can be a complete recipe for disaster for us naturally and spiritually."

Sam just stared at Myra. On one hand, she was intrigued by what her friend had shared because she wanted the bond with Darius, but on the other hand she didn't want any move or word of hers to encourage Myra to keep evangelizing to her.

"I know what's going on in that head of yours. You want me to stop preaching to you as you think I am, but this is really me telling you like it T I is."

"Really? We haven't used that since the 90's." Sam laughed, ragging on Myra.

"Still befitting for now. Seriously, Sam, women are different than men. Look how long it's been since y'all have been together and you still can't get over him. That's because you're a receiver. Women are nurturers by nature and designed and equipped to take in a lot. But men, they're givers. That's even evident with the structure of our genitalia. We have innies and they have outies, if you catch what I'm saying." Myra winked at Sam.

Sam brushed her off with a laugh and the wave of her hand as she went and stood near the window.

"Okay, I'll try to stay serious. For real though, after we're done with them, we're left with a deposit of an array of emotions because we became one with them, but they don't leave the encounter full the way we do. That's why Darius has moved on possibly to another woman's bed while your heart is still tied to him, waiting on him to return."

"You don't know what you're talking about. We may not have been the ideal couple, but I know I meant just as much to him as he meant…means to me. He was open and honest with me about what he wanted, while other guys just play around."

"Sam, just because he told you upfront that he wanted to have sex with you and not serenade you before getting it doesn't make him the one for you. Everyone should be upfront with their intentions. If anything, him telling you that he wanted casual sex with you should've been cause for you to never sleep with him to begin with."

Sam tore her attention from the array of flowered bushes lining the parking lot and scurried to Myra's side. "You are wrong about Darius. Some men are just afraid of commitment because of one bad run in with a woman from their past. I'm going to be the one to show him not all women are the same. Many of us can be trusted." Sam snapped her neck at Myra as she made her way back over to the window. Myra's room position on the front of the hospital gave Sam an angle to see just who was coming in and out of the entrance.

A car pulled up and she squinted and melded her face closer to the window. It looked like she knew the woman getting out of the backseat.

"Sam! Sam! Are you listening to me?"

Sam turned and looked at Myra. "Nope. Gotta go." She clutched her purse as she rushed from the room headed to the front of the hospital.

Sam needed to get to the front to see where the woman Darius was arguing with the past Saturday night at the comedy club was headed.

15

The elevator door finally opened after Sam had been pressing the first-floor button nonstop since she entered on the fourth floor. "Thank God no one else tried to get on," she mumbled to herself. She stepped off and headed toward the glass revolving door at the entrance. She looked from left to right but no longer saw the car outside the front door. She cursed under her breath before turning back towards the elevators.

She looked to her left again and saw the hood of the long tribal patterned cardigan she'd spotted in the car from the window look back down the hallway in her direction. She ducked in an alcove created by two adjoining hospital rooms. When she thought the coast was clear, she peeked her head out of her hiding spot to see the woman was no longer in sight. She practically ran down the hallway looking down each intersecting hallways until she spotted the woman at the final intersecting hallway. She stopped short of it to catch her breath and gather her wits. "What am I doing?" she asked herself as she took deep breaths and stared down at the white tile.

When she finally lifted her head, she noticed the placard on the wall across from her. It had Oncology with an arrow facing the direction that led down the last intersecting hallway. She pivoted her head to the left to see the tribal patterned hood shielding the woman's face as she spoke to a doctor. The woman turned her head and Sam quickly pulled herself out of view.

She stood with her back flat against the wall sucking in deep breaths. "I can either get my tail out of here or see what Ms. Thang is doing here." Seeing as though Sam thought "Ms. Thang" was the reason why she and Darius weren't together, logic evaded her and she peeked her head around the corner again to see that the hallway was empty.

She patted her hair making sure it was kempt and then made her way down the short hall that led to the double doors separating the oncology unit from the rest of the hospital.

She peered through the rectangular window to make sure she wouldn't immediately run into the woman she was referring to as 'Ms. Thang.' When she saw her being escorted into a room a long way down the hall, she pressed the button on the wall causing the massive doors to slowly open.

While nurses and some staff smiled as they passed her by, this wing of the hospital had a different aura than the jovial feeling she had when she was in the maternity ward earlier. She crept to the reception desk.

Although she was a nurse and could probably worm answers from the CAN from that angle, the badge she had in her purse identified her employment at a hospital on the other side of town. She knew there was no logical way to tie in her being a nurse and needing "Ms. Thang's" medical info without raising suspicions. She had to come up with a more plausible story to get the answers she wanted and quick. "Excuse me, I'm here with my cousin, but I had to park the car while she came in. Can you tell me what room she's in so I can go in and be with her?" Sam feigned an air of concern as she looked onto the middle-aged CNA hoping she could get more info on "Ms. Thang".

The woman took her time using her inch-long acrylic fingernails to scratch her cropped hair as she stared at Sam. "What's her name?"

Sam was stumped. How could she find out where the woman was if she didn't even know her name? "Um, um, um…"

"You don't know your cousin's name?" The woman's eyebrow hitched in wonder.

"You know what, never mind. I'll just text her to see where she is."

"Okay, you do that." The woman went back to pecking at the keys on the keyboard in front of her.

Sam made her way over to the sitting area wondering if she should wait it out or leave, but as she stared at the screenshot of her little girl on her phone, she remembered how she wanted Darius and a family with him so she crossed her legs and fell back onto her chair as she waited.

***

After sitting in the waiting area for what seemed like hours to her, Sam was lost on her phone scrolling through Facebook when she heard a doctor talking to the woman with the tribal printed cardigan on and walking towards the reception desk. They stopped a few feet short of it as the doctor pushed the woman's wheelchair. "Kim, you have to stop doing this on your own. You're getting weaker and weaker."

Kim's face was still covered by her oversized hood and her voice was barely audible by Sam, but she had to have said something because the doctor responded to her.

"No, you can still beat this. Like I said, we just have to wait out your treatment and adjust it as needed. And like I've been telling you for a long time, I've seen many patients recover because they drew on the strength of their loved ones to make it through. Tell them now."

Kim's head sank lower into her chest.

The doctor's face was remorseful as she signaled for a CNA to take the woman out.

The CNA who was there when Sam came was leaving and was being replaced by a handsome gentleman. The doctor said something to him and tapped the folder with the woman's info in it as it sat on the countertop. She left it there and walked out with the CNA pushing the woman. The CNA attending the desk nodded his head as he took his seat.

He was slowly pulling the folder from the countertop when Sam rushed over to the desk and leaned over it, causing her elbow to cover the folder, keeping it on the countertop. "Hi there." She hoped that the slow drawl of her words and her breasts peeking out of the top of her V-neck T-shirt would work in her favor. She didn't intentionally do the latter, but if it was working for her, she would play up her 36DD to her advantage.

"Hey." He cleared his throat as he tried to redirect his eyes from her breasts to her face.

Sam took a quick glance at his strong hands and saw that his left ring finger was empty. She was happy that she could proceed with flirting with him. "I've been here before often waiting for my aunt and I've never seen you. I just thought I'd come over while I'm waiting for her and say hi." *Dangit, I told the other CNA I was here with my cousin. Oh well, I never was good at lying.* She dismissed her thoughts as she stared at him

"Hi." He flashed her a toothy smile as he still held on to the folder.

"Are you here at this time often?"

"Yeah, I just got back from lunch and they asked me to relieve my colleague while she takes her lunch."

"So maybe if I come earlier another day, I could have lunch with you?" She batted her long mascara covered eyelashes.

The phone rang interrupting his response. He held his finger up signaling she wait while he took the call.

She winked at him.

"Okay, give me a second." He let go of the folder and spun around in the swivel chair to look into a file cabinet behind him.

Sam seized the moment and quickly opened the folder. Her slanted eyes widened as she scanned Kim's diagnosis and her chemo schedule. Her breath caught in her throat when she saw Kim's potential outcome.

"...okay, no problem." The guy held the phone in his hand as he spun back around.

Sam quickly closed the folder and stepped back from the desk dazed by what she had discovered.

He hung up the phone and directed his attention back on Sam's golden brown face as he finally removed Kim's folder from the high surface of the reception desk and placed it near the phone. He smiled as if he knew she wanted him as much as he wanted her. He stood and walked around the desk and settled next to her as he lowered his voice and whispered. "How about you give me your number and I call you later."

Sam came from out of her trance and looked to her left to see him oogling her. She had what she wanted from him, there was no need to continue the charade. "I'm sorry, I have to go." She turned and sauntered away from him with a new confidence in what could become of her and Darius.

She smiled warily. On one hand, she really did feel sorry for what Kim was going through, but hoping the info on Kim was enough to send Darius rushing back to a healthy, virile woman like herself was enough to forge forth with her desire to get him back. She made it back to the revolving doors of the entrance and dialed his number as she exited. It went straight to voicemail, but that didn't faze her one bit. "Darius, this is Sam. We need to talk." She ended the call and rushed to her car seeking refuge from the brisk fall Chicago winds that sent orange and faded red leaves swirling around her in cyclonic motions. The same way she hoped her revelation to Darius would shift his interest in Kim and cause him to find safety and shelter with her.

16

It was Friday, midday, and Kim hadn't looked in the mirror since Monday morning. Her new ritual of throwing up constantly started after her chemo session that last Thursday. The medicinal marijuana she had been smoking was no longer having a positive effect on her. She woke up that Monday morning honestly readying herself to go to work, but her dance with the toilet proved otherwise. She called in sick and that pattern continued day after day to the point she intentionally missed her chemo session that Thursday.

Of course, the sisterhood, her brother, her mom and dad, and especially Darius had been calling her all week, but she refused to answer her phone or open the door when they stopped by. Her voice was weaker and she knew they would easily detect something was wrong with her if she spoke to them. And although Dr. Ngyuen tried telling her she didn't look so bad after chemo the previous week, she knew anyone who had seen her before would take one look at her and know something was way off with her.

During the week, when she had the strength to, she researched just why the chemo seemed to be doing her more harm than good. In its attempts to destroy the cancerous cells, it damaged healthy ones as well.

She didn't look as bad before she started it, but within the few times she endured it, it literally was sucking the life out of her. Her eyes definitely had lost their vibrancy and they were so sunken in—in contrast to her high cheek bones—that one would swear she had been strung out on drugs for years. She could pinch the skin on her wrist and it didn't snap back into place, it just hung there. As she had seen many times before with other female cancer patients, she definitely needed to wear a wig if she ever planned to set foot out of her house again. Between her thin patches of hair and baby smooth scalp on the other parts of her head, the state of her hair would send the sisterhood into new levels of frenzy if they witnessed the toll the diseases were taking on her body.

You bet Dr. Ngyuen called her that morning asking her why she missed chemo the day before and after moments of Dr. Ngyuen encouraging her not to give up the fight she knew was inside of her, Kim hung up the phone on her. She honestly appreciated the doctor's concern, but her soul was tired.

Maybe if this was her first bout with the dream and hope killer for many, she would fight it until she won, but for her, ten long years of battling it was more than enough. She just wanted it all to be over with.

After the doctor's call, she had turned her phone off. She was tired of the nonstop calls, text messages, and alerts via social media, but she finally decided to turn her phone back on as the end of "General Hospital" played out on TV.

Once it was done calibrating, it registered tens of messages from each of those nearest to her with Darius tallying the most of them all.

She clicked on the voicemail icon and tears stung her eyes as she listened to his deep voice as he questioned her avoidance of him.

She wiped her eyes and spoke to no one but herself. "This is why I never gave my heart to anyone or accepted theirs. The thought of leaving him is too much. Why God, why?" she screamed. She didn't know why but she felt it was necessary.

She'd never questioned Him before, but the more she interacted with, or better yet avoided Darius, the more she wanted to live. She cradled her pillow tight and balled up into a fetal position as the pain in her heart drove her to sleep.

17

Sam had been trying to reach Darius ever since she saw Kim at the hospital the past week, but he had refused to answer or return any of her calls. His refusal to talk to her didn't stop her though. She was privy to his weekly Saturday night gig at the comedy club and opted to take it as her opportunity to tell him there. She wanted him just that bad.

As usual, the lights were dim in the club and a spotlight shone on the stage where Darius was performing. A sly smile tilted the corner of Sam's mouth as she stared at what he physically had to offer a woman—broad shoulders, big strong hands, which she knew exactly how they could drive a woman wild. Big feet. And he was always neat. From the precise lining of his facial hair to his low haircut to how he coordinated his outfits. And the fit of his jeans, although probably not intentional on his part, made a woman privy to the size of his package below. She giggled realizing he couldn't hide it with the baggiest of pants. He was just that endowed.

She licked her lips and slowly swirled her fingertip around the rim of her Sex On The Beach drink, thinking about the last time she was with him. No one, not even Brian, could make her body contort the way it did when she climaxed with him. Although his smile never lingered with her the way hers did with him after sex, she reasoned that he had to really feel something for her to keep coming back to her for five months.

And Darius had admitted to himself that she was the longest he had been with one woman. She had to mean something to him. He'd shown her more affection and attention during their time together than any man ever had since Brian. He meant a lot to her and that was enough to get him back.

Concerned with the lack of humor in his voice, she looked up to see that his face mirrored it as well. It was the third week in a row that he was bombing his set despite him being the funniest man she'd ever met.

She gulped down the rest of her liquid courage. "Yup, I'll tell him as soon as he gets off stage," she mumbled to herself. She switched gears to allow her inner thoughts to roam freely. *If he doesn't already know, he should know. He can't know. The Darius I know would support his woman going through something like that. Like when I got sick that one night he came over. He didn't get mad that he came all the way across town but we didn't have sex because I was so busy throwing up. Nope, he made me soup and tucked me in that night before he left. He checked up on me all day that next day. He was so compassionate and that made me want him even more. He was with me for a stomach virus but not with her for cancer treatments? He's too good of a man not to be there for her, for anyone in that situation for the matter. He can't know, can he?* "But there's only one way to find out." She patted her hair as she hopped off the stool and made her way to cut off Darius's path as he headed for the backroom of the club.

"Darius, can I talk to you for a minute?" Her voice lacked the confidence she thought she would have confronting him. The scowl on his face and shallow pants of his breath gave her pause.

When she didn't speak right away, he brushed past her headed towards his original destination, but her firm grip on his bicep kept him from moving further. "Darius, can I just please talk to you for a second?"

Darius didn't have the desire to talk to her, but he didn't want to make a scene storming off from her. Maybe now that he was face to face with her again, this was his chance to get through to her for once and for all because obviously, the fact that he had been ignoring her calls and texts all week didn't speak loud enough for her.

"Okay, but over here." He moved to the back wall wanting to get out of the path to the bathroom and out of earshot from any patrons. He had received a lot of flack from the bartenders and regulars after Kim had blew up at him weeks back at the club. He didn't want to be the butt of anymore jokes.

The jazz band had taken the stage and Sam hoped that the dissonance of the notes flowing from their first number was not indicative of what was to come with her and Darius.

"Speak." He stared at her as he leaned back against the wall with his mouth tight and forehead tense.

"Darius." The thought of their breakup conversation over a year ago was making her tear up, but she needed to keep her emotions at bay and bare her feelings for him.

She cleared her throat, squared her shoulders, and moved close to him so she could be heard over the music as she continued on. "You said you couldn't be with me because I had too much baggage and came off as too needy, but she has terminal cancer. People like her require a lot of attention. Why her and not me?" The music couldn't drown out the pain in her voice. She refused to wipe her face of the tears that stained it. She wanted him to see just how much his rejecting her hurt. He was the first man she really had imagined a future with after Brian's betrayal. Those after Brian were just placemats.

Even in the darkness, the closeness of his eyebrows showed just how confused he was with what she was saying. "Who has cancer? Who are you talking about?" Darius lifted off the wall. His broad shoulders expanded even more as he folded his arms across his chest.

Sam finally rid her face of her tears. "So you really don't know? That woman you argued with here a few weeks back. The one I heard your friends say you're in love with. I think her name is Kim. Why her and not me?" Sam's eyes glossed over with more tears. She was tired of being the second runner-up to other women vying for the affection of the man she wanted.

Darius's eyes widened. "Kim? How do you know about Kim? And what do you mean she has cancer?" Darius's head was spinning with thoughts of confusion.

"You and your friends weren't all that quiet the day y'all sat at the bar discussing her. My friend was sitting with her guy next to y'all. She didn't catch all of the conversation but she heard enough to know that you really must like this Kim," Sam said, opening and closing her mouth with her tongue grazing it as if the mention of Kim's name left a bitter taste in her mouth.

"Naw, you must be confused. You don't know what you're talking about. Just leave me alone once and for all." Darius tried to storm off but Sam thwarted his attempt yet again.

"I do know what I'm talking about." She kept a hold of his arm and her eyes softened as she looked into his. "I saw her at the hospital when I went to visit a friend..." Sam's words trailed off not wanting to admit that she indeed followed Kim around the hospital, but Darius's raised eyebrow and clenched jaw let her know he expected her to say more.

She acquiesced. "Well, I followed her." Her hands dropped to her sides and she lost eye contact with him, ashamed of admitting her actions to him.

He shook his head and exhaled a frustrated long breath. "You're something else," he mumbled.

Her hands flew up to his chest as she drew closer to him and stared at his strong jawline. His head remained turned away from her. "Darius, I want to be with you. I deserve to be with you. I don't think it was crazy of me to follow her. I just wanted to know what was going on with her. And after I read her chart—"

"You what?" Darius gripped her wrists as he stared vehemently at her.

"Excuse me, man." A short gentleman squeezed past Darius en route to the bathroom.

Darius looked around the dark club grateful that everyone still seemed to be engrossed in the jazz bands performance, but he and Sam had somehow managed to block the path to the bathroom. He pulled her back into the empty corner they stood in just moments earlier when he first tried to get away from her.

Once they were there, Sam tried placing her hands on his chest again, but with a firm grip still on her wrists, he pried her hands off him, released her, and took steps back from her. He shook his head as he rubbed his face in anguish. He felt as if he had aged ten years within the short time he stood there enduring Sam's antics.

He cupped his hands tightly together before rubbing his mouth and preparing himself to speak. He really hoped Sam took heed to what he would tell her next. He towered her as he looked down to make direct eye contact with her.

Sam cowered under his intense stare and stepped back from him some.

"Sam, I really need you to understand that you and I are not for each other. Whether Kim was in the picture or not, you and I still wouldn't be together." He pointed between the two of them.

Sam held her breath as her eyes welled with fresh tears.

Although he had no desire to be with her, he didn't want to hurt her feelings nor make her cry. "I'm not trying to be rude, but I don't know any other way than to be blunt with you right now. You haven't taken all of my other signs and left me alone, so I have to be flat out with you. We were never really a couple, and we won't ever be a couple. I was nervous that time you got sick."

"What?" Sam asked.

He noticed the tears streaming her face and felt like a jerk but he needed to get his point across to her. "Knowing how often we had sex and you throwing up as you did that night made me think you were pregnant. That scared me and woke me up."

She looked confused as she listened to him.

"You knew I didn't want anything serious with you from the beginning, but I thought maybe you were trying to trap me. You know, get me to stay around you if you were pregnant with my child. We were just friends with benefits. I never wanted anything serious with you. I thought you knew that from the beginning."

Sam shook her head in shock.

"Look, Sam, I'm not trying to hurt you with my honesty. I hope like hell you find someone in time that you won't have to chase and do crazy stuff like spy on other women, but Sam, I'm not him. I'm not the one. I gotta go." From the frozen look of hurt on her face and her slumped shoulders, he knew he'd finally gotten through to her. He walked away.

He stormed to the back room of the club discombobulated. He grabbed his jacket hanging on the wall near the back door and headed outside.

He hopped in his car but didn't move a muscle. Although it was cold as one could hear the winds whisking past their ears, he was oblivious to it as he watched his breath fog up the windows. "Cancer?" he said out loud, hoping it would make sense of what Sam told him. "Sam must be confused. Kim, cancer?"

The longer he sat there trying to deny it was Kim's case, the more he thought on how much she coughed when he was around her, how she shivered during game nights while everyone else seemed to be hot from laughing so much. He mindlessly tapped the steering wheel. "Her clothes don't fit her right anymore. Her eyes seem to have lost their sparkle. And she didn't let me touch her like I normally do the last time we were together." He knew something had to be wrong with her. She didn't dominate him in bed the last two times they were together the way she normally would. His last words sent him flying out of his parking space headed to Kim's house.

Darius parked his SUV and was out of it before the engine fully shut down. He made it to her front door in no time flat and commenced to pounding on it and ringing the bell at the same time. He wouldn't let her blow him off this time like she had all the other days he called and texted her. He wanted answers and he planned to get them.

***

Kim had been in and out of sleep all day. The pain suffusing her body just wouldn't give her peace. She slowly sat up in bed wondering if she were still dreaming or if someone was actually pounding at her door.

When she yawned and wiped her eyes trying to adjust them to the light, she knew that it was really someone beating at her door as if they were trying to tear it off its hinges.

She touched her balding head and realized that her scarf must have slid off while she was asleep. Although she didn't plan to open the door and let whoever it was banging on it in, she couldn't stomach walking past a mirror and seeing her hideous reflection. The cancer was attacking her body harder and faster than it ever had before. "Lord please let them leave." She planned to peak out the window and see who was there before making her way to the kitchen to get another bottle of water.

She wrapped her ankle length knitted cardigan tighter around her body. She was getting weaker by the hour it seemed and she didn't know how much longer it would be before she was either forced to check into a hospice or if after months of missing, her family and friends would find her lifeless body rotting in her house.

She took pained, slow steps down the hallway to her living room. She cried knowing if she was her old self, she would have stormed to her door, snatched it open, and tore a proverbial hole in the hide of the fool who continued to pound on it. Only as she got closer to the door did she recognize Darius' worried tone calling out her name on the other side.

She knew she had no fight in her to talk to him so she didn't open the door. Besides, she never wanted him to see her looking the way she did.

She slowly scaled her house holding onto whatever she could for support as she made her way to the kitchen, but a silk scarf laying on the floor stopped her from making it there safely as she fell to the floor.

"Oowww," she screamed out in pain and fear of not knowing if she had actually broken her forearm when she used it to break her fall.

The front door burst open and before Kim knew it a strong hand was caressing her as he spoke to her. "Kim, are you okay?" Her back was to him and the lights were still out so he didn't have a full glimpse of her yet.

She balled up tighter hoping to shield her face from him, but he mistook it that she was in excruciating pain. He quickly engulfed her frail body into his arms as he stood to his feet and rushed to the living room. He gently placed her on the couch, and then went back to try and close the door he thought he broke down making his way into her house.

After he managed to secure it back on its hinges and locked it, he took off his coat and threw it on an empty couch in the living room as he made his way to Kim. He stopped short of her and turned the lights on in the room.

Again, her back was to him and she was balled up. "Kim?" he said in a low yet inquisitive voice as he inched his way over to the couch. He knelt down beside it and began rubbing her back. "Kim?"

She didn't say anything, but the ease with which his finger felt the sinewy bones on her back reminded him of why he rushed over to her house in the first place. His eyes roamed her body and could see right through her long sweater that she was so much thinner than when he saw her last. He took a deep breath and released it slowly hoping that Sam wasn't right.

"Kim, I need you to talk to me," he uttered over her whimpering.

She squirmed, balling up tighter than one would think an adult could. She could feel the scarf shifting on her head and she quickly grabbed the sides of the scarf to keep it in place. She definitely didn't want him to see her head.

"Kim, is it true? Do you have cancer?"

Her body stiffened at his mention of the word destroying her body. *How does he know?* Her whimpers ceased and she laid there as still as she could hoping that death would just swallow her whole. No one was supposed to know, especially not

Darius. *Maybe if I don't say anything or move he'll just leave me alone.*

"Kim, I'm not going anywhere until you talk to me."

She could hear the compassion and resolve in his voice that he wasn't moving from the spot he was in next to her.

He continued rubbing her back with one hand as he slowly guided the other to her head. He wanted to comfort her any way possible. She used to love when he ran his fingers through her hair when they made love, so he thought the action would remind her that she could trust him, but as the weight of his hand lay on her head, she jerked away from him and screamed.

"Get away! Get away, Darius! Leave me alone!" She finally rolled over to face him hoping she could eject venom from her eyes and voice to send him to flight.

The fit she worked herself into had her flailing all over the couch causing her silk scarf to roll off her head. Not having eaten anything in days, in addition to barely drinking water, to throwing up constantly, and the other symptoms of the disease and the treatments she did take, her tirade had depleted her. She could fight him off no more.

Darius sunk to his bottom as he stared at the woman he now knew he loved was absolutely drained. Her beautiful caramel skin tone was replaced with green sagging skin. Her face was sickeningly sunken in causing her normally big eyes to look as if they just sat in the sockets with no facial support around them.

And when he looked at her head, he realized why she lost it when he touched it. He knew Kim prided herself on her looks. She took great care of her lustrous, long, and thick dark brown hair. So, to see barely any there mixed in with patches of baldness shocked him so that his mouth was slightly ajar. His beautiful Kim had been balding and he didn't even know it. He saw the look of sheer horror and hurt in her eyes as she stared at him staring at her and he knew he needed to assure her he still wanted her. "It's okay. We can get through this together." He got back on his knees with his arms outstretched trying to embrace her but she touched her head and realized her scarf was off.

She snapped again screaming and beating his chest until she passed out from sheer exhaustion

Darius was scared beyond comprehension. She appeared unconscious to him as her frail body slumped on his chest. That and her condition caused him to gather her up in his arms and rush her to his car. He had to get her to the hospital and checked out. He reasoned with the way she looked, she had no business being outside of a medical facility anyway.

He ignored the myriad of emotions running through him as he raced over to the hospital. The fear of losing her was at the top of his list, but he knew he had to ignore his feelings. He needed to be strong for her.

He kept looking back at her over his shoulder as she laid balled up on the backseat. She didn't make a sound and that scared him, causing him to speed up.

He got to the hospital faster than he could give the punchline to one of his jokes. He slammed on the brakes as he pulled up right in front of the emergency room entrance doors.

"Sir, you can't park there," an attendant said, walking over to Darius' SUV.

"Tow the damn thing if you need to," Darius belted out as he snatched open the back door and gently lifted Kim's body and cradled it next to his as he hurried into the building.

Unsure of what to do, what to say, or who to go to, he looked from side to side trying to figure out his next move. The receptionist saw that frantic look on his face and ushered him over to her desk.

He made it there and adjusted his grip on Kim as he spoke to the stout woman. "My girlfriend has cancer." His voice broke. "I found her lying on her floor when I went to her house...she fainted."

Seeing a limp Kim draped in his arms made the middle-aged woman come from behind her desk to assist Darius. She flagged down a transporter. "Get a stretcher, ASAP."

She rounded the desk and paged for an attending doctor to come to the ER desk immediately and then directed her attention back to Darius. "Sir, what's her name?"

"Kim." He left it at that staring down at Kim wondering why she hadn't come to yet. She looked so drained. Lifeless.

"Sir, I need her full name."

"Oh, Kimberly Denise Williams."

She began typing Kim's name into the system when the attending doctor came up to the desk. He took one look at Kim and knew she was a cancer patient. He looked up at Darius. "Do you know who her oncologist is?"

Darius was pissed that he didn't have the answer to that question. It was the woman he loved after all and yet didn't even know until that night that she had cancer let alone who her primary doctor was. His head swarmed with thoughts until it landed on the sisterhood. *Maybe Renee or the other ladies would know that. Where are they?* But then it hit him that he hadn't called them to tell them how he found Kim. The longer he thought about it the more he realized that maybe they didn't know she had cancer. With the way they were, it would have somehow come up at one of their many game nights. At the very least, Vance would've slipped him the info.

"Sir," the doctor called out to him, "don't worry about it. The CNA found her primary in the database, and fortunately she's on duty now. We need you to put her on the gurney behind you so we can get her taken care of immediately." The doctor touched Darius's arm causing him to look down.

He saw how tight of a grip he had on Kim's still unresponsive body in contrast to the two attendees behind him waiting to secure her on the gurney.

He hesitantly let her go but not before he kissed her forehead.

It was all too much for him. He had just recently come to terms with the reality that he loved and wanted to be with her and now it looked as if he was going to lose her. *No. I won't. Kim's a fighter. She can get through this. We'll get through this.*

He grabbed her hand as they had finally secured her onto the gurney and started to roll her away.

"Sir, let them take her and I'll have someone guide you to the waiting room in the oncology unit," the doctor said with empathy in his eyes.

Darius' nostrils flared, his eyes became beady, and he clenched his jaws tightly as he stared and towered the five foot four doctor.

The doctor could feel the heat of Darius's nose on his forehead even with the distance between them. He had witnessed enough outcry from grieving family members to know when not to enforce certain rules, not to mention he was honestly intimidated by Darius stature and aura. He understood Darius's grief though and stepped aside to allow Darius to walk with Kim as she was wheeled down the hallway.

By the time they rounded the corners to the oncology unit, Dr. Nguyen was standing in the entryway giving out orders before they even made it to her. "Wheel her into room 3117. And who are you?" She put her hand up stopping Darius from passing her.

He let out an obvious sigh of frustration. He hoped she didn't make it so that she was the second woman he might be offensive to that night, considering that Sam was clearly the first.

"I'm Darius, Kim's boyfriend."

Dr. Nguyen let out a sigh of relief. "She finally told someone."

Darius face contorted in confusion.

She walked off in front of him but spoke to him over her shoulder not wanting to waste any more time getting to Kim. "You wait over there." She pointed to the waiting area. "I'll come get you once I check her out."

Darius took giant, hurried steps to catch up with her. "With all due respect, ma'am, I'm going in that room with Kim and I'm not leaving her side."

She nodded her head in understanding and led him to Kim's room and walked in asking the oncology nurse if she had administered Kim's medicine yet.

When they affirmed they did, she dismissed them and began checking Kim herself and speaking to her.

"Oh Kimberly," she said in her rich Vietnamese accent, "my dear, if you'd only been taking your medicine and coming to chemo like you'd supposed to, you wouldn't be this bad off. I know you're a fighter. You've been beating it for the past ten years. Why did you quit this time?" Dr. Ngyuen spoke aloud to Kim as if it were one of their regular conversations.

Darius's ears perked up and his eyebrows raised in shock. *Ten years?*

"And I think this gentleman here," she looked at Darius over her shoulder and smiled "will help you fight through this if you want to."

The machines beeped as Dr. Ngyuen circled Kim's bed adjusting the levels on the IV bag.

As she was doing so, Darius walked to the other side of the bed and refused to look at Kim's decaying body as he spoke to the doctor. "Doc, is she going to be alright?" He swallowed the large lump of emotions in his throat.

She released the lever on the tube and turned to look at him. "Well," she sighed, "she *is* really dehydrated and malnourished. I'm going to have to run tests on her to see how much more the cancer has spread throughout her body." She paused calculating her next words.

The beeping of the machines was exacerbating Darius already frayed nerves. The pause in her voice and her emotionless face worried him. He just wanted her to give it to him straight.

"When did she tell you and how much did she tell you?"

Darius frowned. He knew the rules, only spouses or parents could get information on patients. He could easily lie to get information from the doctor, but one wrong word from him and she'd know he wasn't fully privy to Kim's state. "Look doc, I'mma be honest with you, she didn't tell me, someone else did. When I went to see her about it tonight, I found her balled up crying on her floor. I talked to her for a minute before she fainted." His voice cracked.

Dr. Ngyuen looked at the vital signs monitor and noted Kim's low stats before turning back to face Darius. Her face was non-telling and she tried to keep the grimness from her voice. "Well, I can't disclose anything to you, but I suggest you get her family here now."

18

Kim's mother and father walked in first arm and arm. Her mother seemed to be providing more support for her husband than he was for her, but if anyone knew them, they'd know that Kim had always been a daddy's girl. Him seeing his oldest child, his oldest daughter, who was once so full of life now struggling to take breaths pierced him to his core.

He made it to her bedside and Andrew, who had come with Renee, rushed and grabbed a chair to put under Mr. Williams to catch him as he had slipped from his wife's grasp. He would've fallen to the floor under the weight of his grief had it not been for Andrew's quick thinking.

Darius flanked one side of Kim's bed. Renee was shielded from seeing her sister until her mother left Darius's side and went on the other side of the bed to be nearer to Kim and try and comfort her. The sounds of the machines were the only things that could be heard in the room until Renee changed that.

Renee took one look at her sister and a piercing wail escaped her before she cupped her mouth and gripped her stomach. Andrew hurried to her, helping her to stand but she beat his chest and screamed before her wails became muffled against his chest and buried herself in it.

He guided her over to a corner of the room and held her.

Mrs. Williams looked up at Darius. "Thank you for being there to find my baby." She reached across the bed to shake his hand.

He obliged, never taking his eyes off Kim.

Dr. Nguyen finally came back in. She scanned the room and walked to stand next to Mrs. Williams. "Hello. I'm Dr. Ngyuen. I've been Kim's oncologist for about ten years."

"Ten years?" Mrs. Williams eyes, just like Kim's, bulged and snapped her neck in shock at the doctor.

"Yes, I take it you're her mother?"

"I am."

"She was first diagnosed with breast cancer right after college. I treated her then and I've treated her through the other times."

Mrs. Williams knees buckled and she held on to the bed rail for support. Pam left Vance's side and went and stood next to her for support.

"I wish I would've met you sooner than today, but Kim wouldn't budge on letting you all in," Dr. Nguyen explained.

Mr. Williams finally stood up and spoke, not caring who saw his shiny face full of tears. "My baby is going to be okay though, isn't she?" He stared right at Dr. Nguyen, avoiding looking at his frail daughter who was stirring in pain.

"Well, we always caught the others early on and the treatment was simple and effective given that it was cancer, but this time—"

"I knew I was gonna die." Kim tried to sit up, but Dr. Ngyuen encouraged her to stay flat against her pillow.

She moved to the other side of the bed with Mrs. Williams and adjusted Kim's bed so it would support her elevated posture. She poured a glass of water and forced Kim to drink it. The fluids they had been pumping in her body obviously had did her some good. She was now lucid, but the doctor could tell from her chap lips that she still needed water.

"Don't say that, sweetie." Mr. Williams rounded the bed and stood next to his wife and rubbed Kim's leg.

"It's true, Daddy. I held off coming to see Dr. N. again, because I just felt in my body that it was different this time. I'm tired." She smacked her lips in between her words. Not because she was trying to be feisty with them, but her mouth lacked the moisture it needed to get out as many words as she had said.

Dr. Ngyuen gave her more water and then grabbed a Q-tip, dipped it in Vaseline, and dabbed some on Kim's lips.

After coughing for a short while, Kim prepared to speak again. "I am tired." Her eyelids fluttered and she coughed.

"Sissy, why didn't you ever tell us?" Renee ran from the corner and jumped in the bed with Kim.

"Renee, get up, your sister needs her space." Mr. Williams chastised Renee.

"That's alright, Dad. We came in this world together and I'm happy now that she'll be here with me when I leave it."

Renee buried her head in between the bed and Kim's shoulder as she sobbed.

The door opened and in walked Keith and Monica. "We got here as fast as we could," Monica said, panting as she rushed to Kim's bedside. She gasped when she finally got a glimpse of her best friend.

Keith soon came and stood next to her. He looked at Kim quickly before turning his head and staring at a wall. His eyes glossed over, all six foot two inches of his body stiffened, and he held his breath as he stared away from her.

"See, this is why I didn't want to tell you all." Kim covered her face with her cover as she whimpered.

"Tell us what?" Monica asked in a high-pitched voice not privy to Kim's condition. She continued to rub Keith's back trying to comfort him.

Dr. Nguyen took the opportunity to speak again. "Kim should be the one to tell you all. But after dealing with her for ten years, I've witnessed firsthand just how stubborn she can be. This time, when the cancer came back—"

Monica gasped and Keith had to hold her up for support as she trembled but he never looked in Kim's direction.

"She didn't come to see me this time until after the cancer had metastasized. I immediately set her up for treatment but she didn't take heed right away."

Mr. Williams tightened his grip around his wife as he listened on about Kim.

"In case you all don't know, while chemo and/or radiation therapy is effective in treating cancer, the latter can weaken the immune system over time. Kim's case called for the highest allowed amount of radiation when she came in so her immune system was compromised quickly. After he informed her about her labored breathing through the night," she pointed to Darius, "and before you all came, I ran tests on her since she hasn't come for her treatments or to see me in the past two weeks and it seems that she got sick, probably from one of her kids when she returned back to work."

"Okay, doc, but she'll be fine once she gets back to treatments, right?" Keith finally spoke up but still never looked in Kim's direction.

"Well, she has pneumonia and with the cancer metastasizing, it's each attacking her body." She couldn't say anymore until tests were done and results were back.

Renee shrieked and tightened her grip around Kim's thin waist.

"But she'll pull through this, right?" Pam asked as she rubbed Renee's back.

"No," Kim said from under the covers.

"Yes, you will," the sisterhood shouted together at her.

Monica walked closer to the head of the bed and grabbed Kim's bony fingers as she held on to the cover to shield her face. "Sweetie, you'll get through this. You have to. You have us all here for support now, and your brother and I need you to spoil the new baby the way you do the twins." She pulled on Kim's hand to touch her two-month baby bump.

Kim pulled her hand back and cried. She would never get the chance to see the twins' graduations and other accomplishments. The knowledge of her not even being at the birth of her triplet's new addition gnawed at her.

Renee squeezed her tighter. "That's right, sissy. You have to stay around for Monica and Keith's new baby and to meet your nephew."

"Hunh?" Kim's voice was muffled by the cover over her face.

"What is going on here?" Mr. Williams spoke up confused at all of the revelations going on while Kim was lying sick in a hospital bed.

Mrs. Williams remained silent praying over her daughter.

"Keith and I just found out today, Mr. Williams. We were gonna have everyone over to the house and share the news, but Kim needs to know now why she has to stick around," Monica said through her tears.

Renee squeezed Kim even tighter as her chin rested on Kim's skeletal shoulder. "And I've just decided that I'm going to do what needs to be done to meet my son. I want to know him and I want him to know me. He can't know me without knowing you too, sissy," Renee said, choking on her tears before she buried her head back on the bed.

"And she will. My daughter is going to be just fine. Right, doc?" Mr. Williams looked directly at her.

"As I said earlier, there's so much working against her body right now." She looked around the room and could see and feel the despair. She knew they were hoping to hear her say Kim would be just fine, but she couldn't guarantee that. "I'll leave you all alone with Kim now while I go order her tests." She squeezed Kim's leg before she walked past the bed and out of the door.

"Come on you all, let's join hands and do what we know to do best, pray," Mrs. Williams directed them.

They grabbed hands, some sniffling, others balling with tears as she began to pray.

"Father God..."

19

Two long weeks had passed since Darius had taken Kim to the hospital. Aside from being forced by Mrs. Williams to go home and shower the third night of him camping out at the hospital with Kim, he never left her side. He had plenty of vacation time saved up at work and planned to use every bit of it to see Kim through her recovery.

Daily, he battled between looking at her and not looking at her. On one hand, it pained him to see her glow fade day by day, but on the other hand, he couldn't help but to stare at her no matter how much she tried to hide her face from him or insist he leave her alone. She was just as pretty to him laying up in the hospital bed as she was when he spotted her across the parking lot at her school's barbecue two summers ago.

It was late in the evening and Darius was in one of his refusing to look at her moments as he sat by himself in a chair in the corner of the room. They honestly had a lot in common, like being candid, their love of old school R&B songs, being self-sufficient, fearless, adventurous, and they both loved sex, just to name a few things, but watching reruns of the 90s sitcom "Martin" had been their solace for the past two weeks. He had brought in his gaming system so they could watch Netflix and Amazon prime via the flat screen TV in the room.

Keith and Renee walked in together. Renee looked over at Darius and gave him a pitiful wave before rushing to Kim's bed and getting in it with her.

"What's up, man?" Keith walked over to Darius to greet him. Darius stood and they exchanged a single-handed handshake as Keith pulled in Darius for a pat on the back. "Thanks for being here with her. We know she doesn't want anyone around but you refuse to leave." Keith tried to inject humor in his voice as he spoke to Darius still leaning into him.

"No problem. She's stubborn as ever, but I know once she gets past this, we'll look back grateful for one another."

Keith finally pulled back from Darius to look him in the face. "You sure do have a lot of faith."

"Hunh?" Darius asked confused.

"I mean faith that her stubborn tail will give you a chance when she gets out of here."

"Oh." Darius chuckled relieved that Keith wasn't like Kim, doubting her recovery from her diagnosis.

"Can you give us a minute? Renee and I want to talk to her alone?" Keith said it courteously, although it really wasn't a question to him. He wanted the time alone with just him and his sisters.

Darius looked past Keith at Kim. She was staring at him, but the minute he made eye contact with her, she looked away. He was reluctant to leave her side, even though she barely talked to him daily. She hadn't flinched on telling him that she didn't want him and that he should just leave her alone. among other flippant things she could manage to say amidst her coughing spells. He knew it was just a facade with her. There were plenty of times over the past weeks he'd been there with her that he'd catch her staring at him when she didn't think he was looking. That look gave him hope for her, for them.

One night she was crying in bed. He didn't know if she was in pain or not, but after the doctors came in and assessed her, he concluded that she was just crying from fear. He begged her to talk to him about it yet she refused. He finally laid in bed next to her in spite of her putting up a fight at first, but he held her tight and kissed her forehead until she finally exhaled a deep breath and fell asleep in his arms. He knew they needed to talk, but he let her resting in his arms comfort them both for the time being.

Keith laughed. "You're really contemplating whether or not you're going to leave? Man, give us some time alone," Keith said in jest as he playfully punched Darius in the shoulder. "You'll be back in here in no time."

Darius looked past Keith again to stare at Kim, regretting having to leave her at all. "Okay, I'll be right down the hall in the waiting area. Better yet, I'll just be right outside the door."

"Alright then." Keith smirked and shook his head in admiration of Darius' dedication to his sister.

Darius left the room and soon Keith was by Kim's bedside. It took a lot for him to come. He hadn't been back since the night she was admitted. He refused to go back not being able to stomach seeing her as she was. He finally looked down at her and his eyes immediately glossed over with tears. She looked even more of a shell of herself than she did before.

Monica and Renee had been pleading with him to go and see her again, but he dismissed them every time. He knew his feisty big sister would pull through in no time and be back to bossing everyone around, but Monica had called him while he was at work earlier that day and told him that Kim really needed to see him and he needed to see her. He knew that much was true.

After breaking down in his office and mindlessly finishing the reports he needed to for the day, he left work, picked up Renee, and they headed over to the hospital. The two of them rode there in silence and now the three of them, born on the same day, from the same womb, just minutes apart, sat in silence together.

Keith sniffled and wiped at his nose with the sleeve of his jacket. He chuckled as he stared at Renee wrapped around Kim's frail body. He said through his tears, "This is the first time, if ever, the three of us have been together and it was this quiet."

Renee managed a half smile but kept her face nestled in the crook of Kim's neck. She didn't care how strong the rancid stench of Kim's medicines were. Being that close to Kim at the moment was the sweetest aroma she had ever encountered before.

In keeping with her routine, Kim was lucid but kept her eyes closed not wanting to see how those around her looked at her. Knowing why Keith hadn't been back to the hospital to see her and hearing him doing a poor job of trying not to cry shattered that section of her heart reserved for their bond.

She was the oldest, their big sister. She was supposed to be strong for them in times of crisis, but she was too weak to barely grip Keith's hand as he had finally locked his fingers with hers. Warm tears covered her face as Renee continued to barely breathe next to her. She knew her sister was trying not to put too much weight on her. God, she wished she could joke about how her not breathing would not change the amount of weight on her, but she was too weak to even joke. She had said less and less as the days went on. In some way, she thought she was saving her wind, her energy for her farewell to them all.

"Renee, get off her," Keith finally said as he pushed at her thigh that was draped over Kim's bony legs. He had looked at his fragile sister long enough and didn't want any extra pressure on her.

"No," Renee uttered.

"Renee!" He raised his deep voice at her.

Kim managed to chuckle at the duo. "It's okay, Keith. You know Renee's always been a hugger."

"And you've always been a fighter. That's why I don't understand why you're not fighting harder to beat this." His voice cracked as he finally buckled over crying. He braced one hand on his knee and his other remained joined with Kim's. When his sobs subsided, he stood again and looked at her. Her big round eyes were shut tight, but the tears steady streamed through the lids.

There was hardly any fat or muscles left on her body. Her face was sunken in and the skin of her cheeks laid lifeless over her bones as if someone had draped a flimsy sheet over an exposed bone. The sight caused Keith to look away from her as he struggled to breathe. His short, shallow breaths reminded him of why he hadn't been back to see her again. To see such a strong woman lying in bed, hopeless, as she was, was too much for him. His sister, his triplet, who never flinched in the face of adversity was visibly weak and speechless. None of it made sense to him.

He calmed his breathing and tried to zone out, but the beeping of the machines providing sources of life and nourishment for her reminded him of where he was and why he was there.

He wiped his face again and squared his shoulders, realizing perhaps he needed to be strong for her. He cleared his throat but his deep, usually smooth voice still wavered as he said, "Kim, I don't get why you didn't tell us all of these years. I could've protected you from it."

His statement temporarily suspended Kim's pain and sadness as she cleared her throat to speak. Renee stared at Keith in disbelief as she grabbed water to allow Kim to sip some through a straw. When she felt Kim had enough, she wiped her mouth with a napkin and nestled herself back to Kim's side and continued to mumble her prayers for Kim's healing.

Kim still couldn't find the courage to look at her brother. She could tell from his shaky voice that he was holding back his tears after his breakdown just moments earlier. She built enough strength to speak. "Protect me from it? It's not like I had a jerk for a boyfriend."

"I know that, but I could've did something." He let out a loud sigh as he pulled the chair near him to sit in it. He kept his hold on Kim's hand and when he had fully taken his seat, he kissed the back of it.

His lips grazing her bones made him pull his face back and stare at her fragile hand. He choked on his emotions as he stared at his tears hitting her hand highlighting the contrast between their hands.

He and Renee shared the same dark chocolate skin tone while Kim was caramel colored in complexion. He was over six feet tall, Renee was visibly taller than her, about five foot seven, and Kim just had to come into the world before them strong and yet small. Her five foot three miniature frame didn't do her life-size attitude and personality justice.

Renee sat up and interrupted the silence in the room. Her throat was raw from having cried since before she entered the room. She interlaced her hand with Kim's as Keith held onto the other one. "Sissy, I can't stop crying seeing you like this."

Kim squeezed her eyes tighter.

"But I know God is a healer. Keith and I were talking on the way over here and truthfully, we're more hurt that you aren̦'t fighting it harder than knowing that you're sick. We know you're going to get past this. We just need you to know that."

Kim couldn't speak. Their bond was strong and she knew they wouldn't understand the gut feeling that she had that this was her last dance with cancer.

"Yeah, Kim. Renee's been praying with the women at her church and Mom around the clock for your healing. If there's anyone that can get a prayer through to God, you know it's Renee." Keith managed to laugh.

Kim gave a half smile as she said, "I hear you all and I thank you for your prayers, but I'm tired."

Keith ignored her declaration. "And you gotta be there when Monica gives birth to our new baby. No one can joke like you while she's going through labor."

"But sissy, you have to meet my son when I square everything away with his adoptive parents and can bring him here from D.C. for a visit," Renee said as if reminding Kim of an agreement they'd made long ago.

"So, you're really gonna seek him out?" Kim managed to get out.

Renee could hear how dry Kim's throat was. She quickly grabbed the cup of water and gave some to Kim. She wanted her sister to talk as much as she could.

"Yes. You being sick made me realize that I have to connect with him. Life is too precious and time is too short." Renee immediately wished she could swallow her words back down her throat as she watched Kim squeeze her eyes tight trying to stave off her tears. It was no use though. Her tears were flowing and her bony chest heaved up and down rapidly as she cried.

"Aw, sissy. I'm sorry for what I said." Renee sank down by Kim's side again and draped her arm across Kim as she cried.

Kim coughed and then said, "Well then at least my dying won't be in vain. I will have done something good with my life. I'll be the catalyst for forcing you to seek out your son." Kim let her head drop to the side as her breathing became even more shallow.

Renee and Keith jumped up at the same time. "Sissy, are you alright?" Renee screamed nervously.

"Kim?" Keith said scared out of his mind that he didn't know what to do to help her.

Kim covered her face with her hands before she composed herself enough to speak. "I'm okay, I'm just upset, wondering if I did some kind of good while I was on this earth."

"Of course you have. You make an impact on those kids day in and day out," Renee said. "And you know you make an impact on the sisterhood. What would we be without you?"

"You've made an impact on me, too." Darius had snuck back in the room and heard Kim's questions about herself.

She squeezed her eyes tight trying to fight off the tears. The mere sound of his deep bass voice, the strength in it when he spoke, pained her chest that she wouldn't ever be able to perhaps give them a chance.

"Kim, you make a difference in everyone's life you encounter," Keith said through his teeth with forced restraint. This was his big sister, although he had always cared for her like he was the oldest. He wasn't letting her go. He jumped to his feet. "Kimberly Denise Williams, I am not letting you go. We came into this world together and while we have no control over whether or not we leave it together, I'm not letting you leave it so soon." His body shook as he sobbed at the thought of her giving up, the thought of her actually dying.

20

Darius and Mr. and Mrs. Williams had just come back in the room after Dr. Ngyuen had asked them to leave so she could speak privately with Kim.

Darius barely slept at all the night before as he made it his duty to study Kim's progress throughout the night. Her breathing was labored and she seemed to wince all through the night from the pain she was suffering.

He had stepped out into the hallway to ask the night nurse if there was any medicine that could alleviate her pain, and she informed him that she was on the allowed amount of dosages for pain reducers.

By that morning, he knew something was different in Kim's body. There was more beeping from the machines and his annoyance of not knowing what was going on with Kim was furthered by Dr. Ngyuen when she showed up first thing that morning and wheeled Kim out for tests. That was all he knew was more tests were being done on her. He hated that Kim had stopped her treatments. Surely it would help and cure her, he thought.

The moment she was reeled out, he jumped on the phone and called her parents to come up to the hospital. He reasoned maybe they could muscle Kim or Dr. Nguyen to share the latest findings on Kim.

Her parents were there in no time. They normally came around noon, knowing that Darius was there with her around the clock and thought his time spent with Kim might actually be good for her, but they came not too soon after he called them at eight-thirty that morning.

Mrs. Williams stood on the side of the bed holding one of Kim's hands as her dad stood on the other side caressing her other hand. He was never embarrassed of crying in front of them about Kim and as much as he wanted to be strong for her, seeing her wasting away as she was hindered his ability to keep his feelings in check.

And as for her mother, she had always been more calm and collect. Her brand of faith in God kept her from falling apart at the sight of her daughter that once favored her physical features. "Kim, I know you're grown and I know your bull-headed tail is so stubborn, but baby, you have to let us in. Update us. Tell us something. Please."

Her mother's plea broke the last of her resolve to keep what Dr. Nguyen had just told her to herself. She pressed the button knowing it would signal the doctor to return.

"What's wrong? You need me to get you something? You in pain?" Darius said as he stared at her with compassion.

She closed her eyes tight trying to wish her tears away. He had been at her bedside day in and day out since she'd been admitted. She tried her best to push him away but he refused to leave her. She wanted not to love him because she thought that would make her transition easier, but holding in how she felt about him seemed to hurt her just as much as the cancer eating away at every cell in her body.

She would hold onto the idea that it would be better to die and have him think she never loved him. She figured he could easily get past that. But if she were to embrace him as she felt and the way he seemed to want her too, she didn't know if he would recover from that loss. She was grateful that death would come soon because the pain of not being with him as she had come to want, or rather realized during her time in the hospital, was destroying her soul the way the cancer was destroying her body.

Dr. Nguyen walked in giving a half smile to Kim's parents and Darius as she walked past them and stood at the foot of the bed next to Kim. Darius moved to stand next to Kim's mother. Her height, skin tone, and facial features reminded him so much of Kim. It was comforting to be near her.

"You're giving me permission to tell them, right?" Dr. Nguyen asked Kim for clarity recounting the conversation they had in the room after they discussed her lab results.

Kim didn't have the energy to share the news with anyone if she decided to and she knew she didn't have the heart to tell them. She squeezed her eyes tight and nodded her head.

Dr. Nguyen gripped the rail on the footboard with one hand and clasped Kim's charts on a clipboard in her other hand. "Mr. And Mrs. Williams and Darius, from what Kim has told me and I've witnessed over the years, none of you all know what types of cancer she's battled with. She was diligent with her treatments with her first three diagnosis of cancer. Many side effects of cancer treatments go away fairly quickly, but some might take months or even years to go away completely. In Kim's case, there seems to have been some damage to her kidneys, but it's only just become visible to us. Also, certain types of treatments sometimes cause delayed effects, such as a second cancer that may show up many years later. That later is now. The cancer has rapidly metastasized in the upper region of her body. The masses and tumors are pressing against her organs and affecting their functioning.

"If we would've caught them earlier, perhaps chemo or radiation therapy could've helped, but the little chemo she's taken since her recent diagnosis hasn't helped to shrink the masses yet. The chemo treatments she's taken over the years did weaken her immune system to a degree, and when she got pneumonia, it further damaged her organs." She walked to the head of Kim's bed to point out some machines. "Kim's liver fatally decreased its functioning last week due to the effects of the treatments over the years and tumors pressing against it and so this machine has been doing its job." She touched the machine acting as a liver for Kim. "And after Darius complained about her breathing pattern last night, I took her in for tests today to find out that her respiratory system is failing her. The thymus cancer is back and the mass has compromised the functioning of her lungs." She paused as she waited for Mr. Williams to go stand by his wife's side.

"If it were maybe one organ, we could put her on the list for a transplant, but with the cancer spreading the way it has, she's not a candidate for a new liver."

"So, what are you saying, doctor?" Darius's voice was strained.

"We'll do everything we can to make sure that she is comfortable while she's here, but—"

"But what?" Mr. Williams' voice quivered with anxiety and fear.

"There's not much else we can do for her. And she wanted me to tell you all that she signed a DNR."

"A DNR. What's that?" Mrs. Williams asked as she gripped her husband's hand and Kim's at the same time.

"A DNR means do not resuscitate. Kim does not want you all to keep her on life support or try to save her if it comes to that."

A squeal escaped Mrs. Williams's mouth before she brought her hand up to it. She closed her eyes and took a deep breath. "Thy will be done, oh God," she said aloud, trying to calm her nerves and stay grounded in her faith.

"So what are you saying, Dr. Nguyen?" Darius asked heated.

"Kim's organs that are necessary for life are shutting down on her."

"No. My baby is a fighter. You can beat this, Kimberly." Her dad lowered his head until his forehead rested on hers. His tears blended with hers as they hit her face and trickled down it.

"I'm tired, Daddy." Her weak declaration escaped her dry throat.

"No, baby girl. You have to make it through this. You have to." His body jerked as he cried.

His wife rubbed his back as she sang a hymn that she used to sing to her kids all of the time when they were younger.

Her mother's strong yet calm voice made Kim sob even more so than her father. It was sinking in that she would never hear her mother sing to her again. She squeezed her mother's hand tighter. *Why couldn't I have faith like my mother?*

Darius' voice interrupted her internal thoughts. "There has to be something we can do, right?"

"Just spend as much time with her as you all can," Dr. Nguyen said.

"How much longer?" Darius didn't know where he found the audacity to ask the question. He was prepared to fight with Kim to stay alive, but the question bubbled inside of him and came out before he knew it.

"I suggest you have the rest of the family visit her today," Dr. Nguyen said in a grim voice before excusing herself from the room.

Darius stopped breathing as it registered to him what Dr. Nguyen was implying.

Mrs. Williams wiped the tears from her face as she rubbed her husband's back. She looked down at Kim. "You know the Lord is with you and loves you no matter what, right?"

Kim squeezed her eyes as tight as she could, trying to block out the sight of her mother. She was so beautiful in her sorrow trying to invoke hope.

"I know He loves me, Momma, but I strayed away from Him."

"But He's always waiting with outstretched arms for you to walk back in to. It's never too late, baby. Repeat after me, Father God, I come to You with a broken spirit and contrite heart, but You're faithful enough to forgive me of my sins and cleanse me from all unrighteousness..." By the time Kim had repeated every word her mother said, Mrs. Williams was chest to chest with her daughter as she hovered over the bed embracing her. She hadn't shed a tear and she wouldn't in front of Kim. She merely placed a long tender kiss on Kim's cheek before she stood upright again. She squeezed Kim's hand and smiled at her although her daughter's eyes remained shut tight as she battled her cries.

Mrs. Williams looked back at her husband and cleared her throat before speaking. "Gerald, it'll be okay. I'm gonna step in the hallway and call Renee and Keith at work. I'm certain Keith will tell Monica and Monica will tell Pam to come here, too." She breathed a deep sigh as she walked past Darius and squeezed his arm. She could tell he was in just as much shock as anyone could be given what Dr. Nguyen had implied.

***

Kim's breathing was labored as she lay in bed covering her face from those around her. Keith, Monica, Pam and Vance had finally made it there and all eyes were focused on her. She asked them to dim the lights in the room. She didn't want them to see her go out like that. She had always prided herself on her looks. She didn't want anyone's last memory of her to be that of her sunken in cheeks and eyes, her balding head, her putrid color, or her rail thin frame.

Renee lay in bed nestled next to her with her head buried in the crook of her neck and her arm draped over Kim as she wept silently.

Kim desperately wanted to console Renee as her body heaved up and down next to her, but she just didn't have the strength and energy to do so. It killed her to know that she would no longer be around to protect her sister. She felt there was so much more she needed to be there for her for, but she found herself smiling knowing that if Renee and Andrew did work out as a couple, Renee would be in good hands.

Monica and Pam wanted to flank Kim opposite of Renee when they came into the room, but Mr. and Mrs. Williams occupied two seats next to Kim's bedside. Monica and Pam chose to stand next to Renee and hold onto any part of Kim they could. They needed her to feel their touch and know they were there for her.

Vance stood behind Pam. Not only was he there to support his wife, but he'd known Kim as his employee long before he met Pam and he knew it was good for him to be in the room to support his best friend Darius as well. Kim's sickness weighed heavy on him as her boss and her friend.

Everyone around Kim aided in the emotional agony she was experiencing as she lay helpless in her bed. She didn't want them to see her and suffer knowing they would soon lose her.

Darius, wanting to be as close to her as possible, but outranked by people who had known her longer, had no choice but to sit at the foot of her bed. He tried rubbing her feet as a means to be close to her, but after several attempts of her trying to pull away from him, he decided he didn't want to cause her any extra discomfort. But he wanted to, needed to, touch her. He thought maybe if he did, she could feel his love in his touch and fight for them.

Renee's cries subsided long enough to look up and around the room for Keith. When she didn't spot him, she broke the pain-filled silence crowding the room. "Where is Keith?" She swallowed the emotions in her throat.

"In the hallway," Monica said through her tears.

"He needs to be in here," Renee said angrily and jumped up from the bed.

Andrew came out of the shadows of his corner and was headed to Renee but Monica held her hand up to stop him as she held Renee down. "Renee, you know how he feels about seeing her like this,"

Monica said softly, trying not to further disturb Kim's restless body.

"I don't care how he feels. We should all be in here together huddling around Kim giving her strength and letting her know we need her here." Renee turned her attention and anger to Kim. "Kim! Kimberly!" she shouted at her.

Mr. Williams stood up. "Renee, what is wrong with you? Stop shouting at her."

Renee ignored her father and straddled Kim as she looked down on her. She could barely breathe and see through her tears as she continued her tirade with her triplet, her best friend. "Kim, fight." She reached down and grabbed Kim's shoulders. "Fight."

Andrew and Darius stood next to each other, both unsure of whether or not Mr. or Mrs. Williams would stop Renee or if they needed to get Renee off Kim.

Pam and Monica were shocked at Renee's outburst, but they also understood her emotions behind it.

"Kim, fight." Renee continued to shake her.

"Renee, baby, it's going to be okay one way or the other, but you can't do her like this." Mrs. Williams stood up as she caressed Renee's back.

"Kim, fight," Renee screamed again through her tears.

Keith rushed through the door and to Kim's bedside. "What is going on in here?" His eyes were bloodshot red and he was out of breath panting from his sprint into the room.

"Sissy, fight." Renee continued shaking Kim.

The sight of his sister's skeleton sheathed with sagging skin, her mouth gaped open trying to utter words to Renee yet crying relentlessly infuriated him. He lurched forward and snatched Renee off Kim's body by her upper arms.

Although she was 5'8" and about 150 pounds, her feet dangled above the floor as he held her up in the air and shook her as if she was a rag doll. His regimen of working out was apparent as his biceps and triceps flexed and the wings on his back spread wide as he shook Renee in the air. His 6'2", solid frame easily upheld hers as he said, "What is wrong with you?" His eyes showcased hurt and rage.

"What's wrong with me? What's wrong with you?" She flailed in his arms trying to break free of his grasp.

"Put your sister down now," Mrs. Williams demanded of Keith.

Andrew now stood near the sister-brother duo with his fists balled and his jaws clenched. He wasn't sure if he should interrupt the interaction between the two, but his desire to protect Renee from anyone and at any cost drove him to do so. He would fight her brother if he needed to and unfortunately, even at a time like the present. "I know she's your sister, but she's my woman. Please take your hands off her now."

Keith had already ignored his mother's request, so ignoring Andrew's was just as easy. He stared into Renee's eyes. "What's wrong with me? I come in here to see you over Kim and shaking her. Look at her! Look at her!" His voice trembled as he turned

Renee's body, still in his hands, to look at Kim whimpering yet looking so fragile. She looked as if she could break at any moment. "Look at her." His last statement was barely intelligible as he pulled Renee into him.

She knew he would never truly hurt her and her arms locked around his neck as his hands fell to his side.

Her feet touched the ground but she never let go of his neck as his body lowered to adjust to her feet being flat on the ground.

He finally wrapped his arms around her and others in the room couldn't tell where his cries ended and hers began.

"It's okay, babies." Mrs. Williams rubbed Keith's back as Mr. Williams drew closer to them and rubbed Renee's back, all the while still squeezing his wife's hand.

Kim's wheezing and apparent need to get more oxygen hushed the room and they all turned to face her. It looked as if she was convulsing and the monitors on her machines were beeping erratically.

A nurse rushed in. "Excuse me." She pushed past the barrage of people surrounding Kim's bed and began to check her vitals. The beeping on the machines soon slowed down and she turned to face them all. "I know this is a trying time for you all, but with her limited capacity to breathe on her own, whatever was just going on in here is too much for her right now."

"We're sorry. We'll try to keep her calm," Monica said through her tears.

"Thank you." The nurse gave them a sincere smile and patted Kim's arm who was still crying, and then she left the room.

Mr. Williams went back to Kim's side and began to stroke her head and kiss her forehead trying to comfort her.

Pam and Monica were on the other side of her bed holding her hand and each other's. Monica hummed a song of worship in her ear.

Keith finally stood straight up and reached behind his head to loosen Renee's grip on his neck. She merely replaced her tight hold around his neck to around his waist and buried her head on his chest as she continued to cry.

"Renee, I'm sorry. I would never hurt you but when I came in and saw you on top of her shaking her, I lost it."

"I know, Keith," she mumbled on his chest. "But you should be in here with us. Not hide from her as you have been."

Keith interlaced his hands on top of his head and blew out a loud breath willing himself not to cry or break down again. When he felt he had the tremors in his voice under control, he spoke again, but it still shook with agony. "I just can't sit in here with y'all around her and watch her waste away. She's one of the strongest women I know and to see her like this…" He extended his hand out pointing at her. He and Kim made eye contact. It was as if her eyes told him she was sorry. He pulled his bottom lip in trying to stop the wail he knew was brewing in him but the lone tear trailing down Kim's face as her head laid to the side caused him to push Renee off him and he buckled over wailing.

"My God," Mrs. Williams called out a she held her tears in. She had decided from the moment she found out Kim's diagnosis that she would have to be the strong one for them all. She knew the time would come soon enough where she would grieve as only a mother could from the pain she saw her daughter suffering, but she knew that time wasn't now.

Renee draped herself over Keith's back as she sobbed along with him.

Monica was readying herself to go to her husband's side, but Renee stood straight up, wiped her face with the long sleeve of her flannel shirt, and then grabbed her brother's hand and forced him to stand up, too.

His body jerked as he had no control over his cry, but she placed her hand over his chest and began praying as she normally did. She stood on her tiptoes so that the whisper of her voice could better reach his ears through his crying. "Come on, Keith. This hurts but we have to be strong. God knows I don't know how to right now, but let's at least try."

Keith pulled in one more sniffle and let Renee lead him over to Kim's bed.

They made it to her side and their father stepped out of the way knowing the trio needed a moment together.

Renee spoke up first. She rubbed Kim's forehead. "Sissy, we know you keep saying you're tired, but we need you to fight to stay alive. Look, everyone around this room loves you and is rooting for you." Renee looked at Kim and then looked around the room at Pam and Monica near each other. Monica shed tears as her hand reached across the bed and gripped Keith's hand.

Pam's face was wet from crying since she'd gotten the call earlier that day. It sent her rushing to the hospital straight after work. Vance stood behind her with his arms secured around her waist with a somber look on his face.

She refused to look at Darius at the foot of her bed and instead looked at Andrew with a look of confusion on his face. He paced a little in the spot he stood in. She figured he wanted to be by Renee's side so she smiled as best as she could and nodded her head at him in Renee's direction. He understood what she was silently telling him and rounded the bed as fast as he could. "Excuse me." He squeezed past Mr. Williams and took up residence next to Renee. He placed a soft kiss on her cheek before locking his arm around her waist.

Kim took a deep breath to talk as loud as she could as she stared directly at Andrew. She cleared her throat. "My sister never told us what's going on between you and your family but whatever it is please make it right so you can share your life with my her." Renee wiped at her tears as Kim cleared her throat again and took another deep breath. "I know she wants to share hers with you."

Renee battled her cries as Andrew squeezed her tighter.

Darius's eyes widened as he stared at Kim and ignore the fact that there were others in the room or what was happening with her for that matter. "So you can give him advice to make things right to be with your sister, but you can't be honest with me about your feelings and accept mine?" Darius cocked his head and huffed as he stared at Kim.

Vance walked up to him. "Come on man. Leave that alone. Now is not the time for this."

Darius stared at Vance. "No man, this is the best time for this." Darius took steps towards Kim who was shaking her head with her eyes closed, but Mrs. Williams pleading eyes as she looked into his, made him stop in his tracks. He rubbed his face in angst.

Kim finally opened her eyes again. Even with the lights dim in the room, Kim could see everyone and her attention was drawn to her mother. She had always admired her mother for how strong she was and she saw it now as she stood at her bedside. She could see that her eyes were glossy but her face was dry. She hadn't seen her cry at all that day. It didn't offend her because she'd inherited the trait of being strong from her mother. But her father, he was a different kind of strong.

He was strong in his values, strong in providing for them, and strong raising them up in God, but he never held back on showing his emotions when it came to their triumphs and tragedies. And if ever there was a tragedy in their family, the possibility of losing his oldest daughter is what kept the tears streaming down his face.

There was still that one person in the room that Kim refused to look at—Darius. She couldn't handle the emotions attached to his stares.

"Sissy, sissy. We need you to fight," Renee said, bringing Kim's attention back to her.

Kim looked at Keith and then at Monica. "Babies." She choked on her words causing Renee to panic.

Renee grabbed water for Kim as Mrs. Williams and Pam's prayers grew louder.

When Renee was satisfied that Kim was no longer choking, she pulled the cup from her lips, sat it down, and stroked Kim's head as she intermittently kissed her forehead.

Kim looked past Renee at Keith and Monica. "Babies." She uttered again.

With Renee's ears closer to Kim's lips, she understood what she said and sprang upright quickly. "She said babies. Mon and Keith, I think she's asking about the twins."

Kim nodded and squeezed her eyes as she cried. She hated normally being the most vocal one out of the entire room and yet someone now had to speak for her to be understood.

Monica wiped the tears on her pronounced cheeks and gripped Kim's hand even tighter.

"They're with Monica's mom. You'll see them soon, once you're better." Keith cleared his throat.

Kim squeezed her eyes tighter and shook her head from side to side as strongly as she could. She may not have been able to speak, but she could play the heck out of charades. She needed them to see the picture that she could only paint with her head gestures. She vehemently shook her head from side to side.

Keith first understood what she was saying without actually saying it. "Oh yes you will see them later. You are getting better. You're getting out of here, alive and well."

"Yes, sissy. You'll be a testimony to others that God can do anything."

She was tired and she realized they would never accept what she was saying, so she stopped trying to get her point across. She calmed herself in the bed the best she could and closed her eyes.

Everyone stared at her.

Darius finally spoke up. "She still breathing, right?"

Keith's head dropped and bobbed on his chin as he cried and his shoulders slumped. Monica came from her side of the bed and to his side to comfort him.

Everyone in the room seemed to turn to their mates for comfort, all but Darius. Kim completely turned over on her side trying to get as far away from him as possible. Her body jerked as she cried into the pillow.

"Excuse me, excuse me, excuse me." Darius brushed past everyone on Kim's bedside until he was at the head of her bed and interrupted Renee from rubbing Kim's forehead.

He leaned down until his forehead touched the side of her face and rubbed her head as he talked to her. "Kim, fight for us. I love you." He placed a tender kiss on her cheek and his lips remained there until he noticed something. He jumped up. "She's not breathing." The alarm in his voice rang out just as soul piercing as the long steady beep on the machine monitoring her heart beat. "She's not breathing." He looked around at everyone who seemed to be holding their breaths.

Dr. Ngyuen came in the room with two other nurses and stood at the foot of the bed. "I'm sorry you all." She looked at Mr. and Mrs. Williams. "I'll give you a chance to say your last goodbyes."

"Goodbye? So what, y'all just gone give up like that?" His deep voice bellowed out in the room as he threw his hands up in the air. His eyebrows furrowed as he stared at each of them. "Y'all just gonna give up?" He looked at a few around the room frozen in sheer disbelief of what had just happened. "Do something," he screamed at the doctor. "Do something. Save her."

"Darius." Vance looked to him as he caressed his weeping wife's back. Pam's petite body clung to his muscular frame as she sobbed on his chest.

Darius ignored Vance and turned to hover over Kim again. "Save her. Wake up, Kim. Come on, baby. Wake up. Don't give up on us." His voice cracked with the last of his words as his body heaved on top of Kim's. "Do something, Doc." He squeezed Kim's hand as he caressed the side of her face with his.

"I'm sorry, Darius. She signed the DNR. There's nothing more we can do," Dr. Ngyuen said.

Andrew, not too far from Darius, had to pick Renee up from the floor. She had been holding her breath when Kim flatlined, but after hearing the doctor's statement, she fainted.

"Just take deep breaths, baby. Take deep breaths." Monica was trying to overcome her tears and pain as she worked to calm Keith since he was hyperventilating. She finally got him to brace his hands on his knees as he was bent over and pull in deep, slow breaths.

"Nooooo. No, no, no." Mr. Williams dropped in the chair behind him.

Mrs. Williams squeezed her husband's hand. "Earth has no sorrow that heaven cannot heal." She mindlessly mumbled the words of the song seeking comfort in God.

"Kim, baby, wake up." Darius gathered her lifeless body in his arms and kissed her cheek. He knew she wasn't affectionate with him outside of them having sex and he hoped his pecks on her face would cause her to awake and berate him for his public display of affection, but she never said anything as he continued to plant kisses on her face.

Vance had come up behind Darius. "Come on, man, let's take a walk." He tugged on Darius's arm to pull him away from the bed but Darius snatched his arm out of Vance's grasp. "No. She's just asleep. I have to be here when she wakes back up." He looked down at her. "Why you gotta be so stubborn, hunh? Just wake up already."

Dr. Ngyuen and her staff had walked up to Kim's bed opposite of Darius and paused.

"Darius, she's gone." Dr. Ngyuen reached across the bed and touched Darius's arm.

He heard her words, but it wasn't until he looked down at Kim again to see her motionless in his arms, eyes closed, and mouth gaped open that the truth began to sink in. He couldn't feel her heartbeat against his chest as he had done so many times before when he'd collapsed on her after they'd made love.

The weight of Dr. Ngyuen's words hit him. It was as if someone had laid an hourglass on its side and stopped time.

He softly laid her back down on the bed and kissed her lips one last time before he stepped away from her bed.

"Come on, let's step outside for a second," Vance suggested to Darius.

"Leave me alone." Darius's voice was full of malice as his nostrils flared and he stared at him. He brushed past Vance and stormed out the room.

He walked out into the hallway, furious at seeing a huddle of people outside of another patient's room laughing. His world had just come to a perilous halt but everyone outside of Kim's room was carrying on with life as if a beautiful soul hadn't just perished.

He mumbled expletives under his breath as he stomped down the hallway with balled fists.

Vance caught up to him by the time he made it to the oncology exit leading to the front of the hospital. "D, bro. Wait up. Just give me a second to check on Pam and I'll take you home." Given Darius's bloodshot red eyes, puffed cheeks, and clenched jaws, Vance didn't know how Darius's state of mind would translate into him getting home safely.

"I said leave me alone, Vance."

"Naw, man. I gotta make sure you're straight."

Darius found Vance's words oddly funny. He chuckled as he turned to fully face Vance. "Am I straight? Hell naw, I ain't straight, man. This is my fault."

Vance's eyebrows crinkled as he stared at Darius. "Your fault?"

"Yeah. Her death, losing her has to be payback for the way I've treated women over the years."

"D, you're not making any sense."

"It makes sense to me. Not that I was a dog cheating on women, but the fact that I never settled down with any of them probably broke so many of their hearts. This is my payback." His voice was raw with emotion as he pointed back towards the hospital.

"D, that's not true."

"Oh, it isn't?" With raised eyebrows, he leaned into Vance. "So why is it that when I finally decide to love a woman, I mean really love a woman, she ups and leaves me?" he asked, staring at Vance. He laughed and shook his head as tears rolled down his face.

He turned and leaned on the door of his SUV and let out a loud huff before he kicked his car.

"Darius, take it easy, man." Vance grabbed Darius on his shoulder, but he shirked him off.

"Just leave me alone." Darius never looked back at Vance as he somehow simultaneously unlocked his car, jumped in it, and sped off, swerving out of the parking lot.

21

Andrew's bulky arms cradled Renee close to him. She still hadn't come to. He was still in shock of the loss of Kim but he knew that he wasn't that far out of it to do what he was thinking. He'd seen how people on TV and in the movies slapped someone in the face to wake them up after passing out, but he wasn't sure if it really worked, nor did he want to touch his earthly angel like that. Her chest rising and falling let him know that she was still breathing so he pulled her close to him to whisper in her ear. "Renee, please wake up. I need to know that you're alright." He kissed her cheek.

She stirred in his arms and he breathed a deep sigh of relief.

She sat upright in his arms and rubbed her face as she looked at him. "Thank God. I had a dream that we were at the hospital and Kim had died. I'm so glad it was just a dream." She hugged his neck but soon looked past him to see Monica holding up Keith who was still sobbing against the wall. Her eyebrows furrowed as she turned to her left to see her mother standing over her seated dad rubbing his back. She heard someone sniffling behind her and when she snapped her neck to see who it was, she saw Pam hovering and crying over a hospital bed. She turned to look back at Andrew. "Where are we? Where am I?"

She looked into his despondent eyes hoping that he wouldn't say what was coming back to her. His downtrodden eyes alarmed her and she quietly turned herself away from him and braced her hands on the side of the hospital bed. She slowly rose from the floor until she became eye level with Kim's closed eyes and gaping mouth.

The sight was too much. She let out an earsplitting scream as she stood to her feet and began to shake Kim. "Sissy, wake up. Stop playing."

Kim's lifeless body only moved because of Renee's forceful shoves.

Andrew quickly rose to his feet and grabbed Renee by her waist. "Come on, Renee, let's go for a walk."

"No." She tried to escape his grip. "No, Kim is just joking with us. She'll wake up any minute."

Mr. Williams' whimpers grew louder.

"You know what you all, let's leave. Staying here and watching her won't make her come back, and obviously, it's not good for us right now." Mrs. Williams took a deep breath and began to help her husband stand.

Vance walked back in and went to Pam's side.

"No, Momma. I'm not leaving Kim." Renee stared boldly at her mother.

"Keith, get your sister and let's go." Mrs. Williams looked to her son. The tone in her voice left no room for defiance on his part.

Keith pushed himself off the wall with his foot. Monica elevated on her tippy toes and kissed his cheek as she rubbed his chest. She wiped at the tears flooding her face as he walked away.

Andrew stepped back by the time Keith made it to him and Renee.

"Come on, Renee, let's go." His deep voice sounded crushed.

She turned to face him. "No."

"Come on, sis." He wrapped his arm around her waist and pulled her towards the door.

She quickly latched on to the side of Kim's bed. "No. Let me go."

Keith didn't say anything. He squatted a little, wrapped his arms around her waist, and picked her up kicking and screaming. "Renee, I know you're hurt, but we'll get through this together."

By the time they made it to the door of the room, Renee's voice was inaudible and she looked like a ragdoll suspended in Keith's arms. She was weak and had given up on fighting him. He put her down on her feet as he opened the door.

She wrapped her arms around his waist and clung to him as they cried and walked out of the room together.

Monica grabbed her purse and followed them out with her head hung low.

Andrew, Vance, and Pam left out right after Monica.

Mrs. Williams walk over to Kim's bedside and lowered her face until her lips pressed against Kim's stilled forehead. Her emotions clogged in her throat as she rubbed her first born's head, but hearing her husband whimpers grow louder and louder reminded her she had so many people to be strong for. "Bye, baby. I will always love you." She pressed her lips against Kim's forehead one last time before standing upright again. She wiped her face free of her tears and turned to face Dr. Nguyen and her husband. "Thank you." She nodded at the doctor and then helped to brace her husband as he stood.

His knees wobbled as he made his way to the door, but luckily, Andrew lingered near the door and helped Mrs. Williams usher him to their car.

Thankfully they didn't look back as the nurses began to turn off the machines that once helped to sustain Kim's life.

22

"You sure you wanna do this now?" Renee sniffled as she held the phone up to her ear.

"Yeah, I wanna honor Kim's wishes," Andrew said as he closed the door to his car.

"Thank you so much," Renee said between her cries.

"Don't worry, I'll handle this real quick and get back over there to you at your parents' house."

"No rush, take your time." She took a deep breath.

"No, I'll be there soon. I wanna be there for you in your time of need."

"Thanks."

"I'm here now. I'll call you back when I'm on my way."

"Okay. I'll say a prayer for you." Her voice was flat.

"Renee, thanks. See ya soon," Andrew said to the dial tone. She hung up before she heard the last of his statement. He knew her heart was broken and couldn't wait to get back to her, but he needed to handle this part of his life first. He put his phone in his pocket and found himself standing at the door of his adoptive parents' home. He had escorted Renee to the car with her parents after they left out of the hospital, but had talked to her on the phone his entire ride there.

He still had his key to the house but he hadn't used it since before he found out that his adoptive father, Charles, was really his biological father and had raped his biological mother back when she was a student in one of his classes. The trauma of being raped and having to give birth to the baby ate away at his biological mother, Marie, until she finally decided to give Andrew up for adoption when he was four. He hadn't found out all of those details until the past year or so when he discovered that his then girlfriend, Melanie, was also Marie's daughter, making her his sister.

Luckily for Andrew and Melanie, they never were intimate with each other. But all of the details of how Andrew came to be forced him to stay away for months from the family that had raised him. Not only was he disgusted with his father for raping Marie, but he also found out that Charles had known for years that Andrew was his after seeing just how much alike they really looked and the knowledge that they each had the exact same shape, color, and size birthmark in the same location.

He rang the doorbell and knew he would be a surprise to whoever opened the door.

"Coming."

He could hear his adoptive mother, Elizabeth, walking towards the door. She opened it and tears sprang in her eyes as she cupped her gaping mouth trying to quell her shock of seeing Andrew after he'd stayed away from her for so many months.

"Hi, Mom." He hated that he had managed to make her cry every time he'd been around her the past year, but tonight, he'd put an end to that. "Can I come in?"

She snatched him by his wrist into the house and right into her arms. "Andrew, I am so happy to see you, baby. You don't ever have to ask to come home, just do it." Her words were barely intelligible through her sobs.

He returned her embrace just as tight as hers and took a deep inhale reacquainting himself with her welcoming vanilla scent. It was her signature and added to the warmth she exuded over the years. He cursed himself inwardly for staying away from her as long as he did while avoiding his dad, Charles. "Ma, is Charles here?"

"Yes." She hesitantly pulled back to look at him. Pleased that he no longer looked disheveled and stressed as he had the last couple of times she saw him, she finally smiled at him before kissing his cheek. "You wanna see him?" She looked at him with worry in her eyes knowing the last few times they interacted with one another, it ended up with either of their jaws swollen and bruised bodies.

"Yeah, I do."

"Okay." She locked her elbow with his and guided him toward the family room where Charles was watching the Discovery Channel.

Charles was already standing on his feet by the time they made it to the doorway. He too remembered his last encounters with Andrew and he needed to have his feet grounded to handle his former attacker, if necessary.

Andrew paused before entering the room and simply stared at Charles. He definitely had aged. Just last year and being in his early sixties, Charles still had a head full of black hair, but Andrew could now see specks of gray sprinkling his head and his hairline was receding. He had bags under his eyes. And he had lost weight. His physique wasn't as solid as it used to be. He didn't look the same to Andrew anymore.

"Charles, Dad," Andrew said in a faint voice.

"Andrew." Charles' muscles tensed.

"Relax, Dad. I just came to talk."

Charles exhaled a deep breath and revisited his seat seeing Andrew's relaxed demeanor as he stood across the room from him. "Have a seat."

Elizabeth's smile widened with the realization that two of the most important men in her life were actually going to have an adult-like conversation after the year they had. "I'll leave you two alone." She turned and was headed on her way back to the kitchen, but Andrew stopped her in her tracks with his words.

"Mom, please stay in here. What I have to say needs to be said to you as well."

"Okay." Elizabeth bore a pensive face as she went and took a seat next to her husband.

Andrew released a slow exhale and rubbed his face quickly mentally reliving the past couple of hours he spent at the hospital. It reminded him of the importance of him being there sitting across from the people who had raised him, nurtured him, cared for him when Marie had given him up.

He looked at Charles first. "I've been avoiding you all, mainly you, Dad, and you all know just why. It still sickens me to know that you raped Marie."

Charles tried to interrupt Andrew, but he was silenced with the lift of Andrew's hand. "I really don't wanna hear your explanation again for why you did it or why you omitted to tell me that you knew you were my biological father for so many years upon your discovery of our matching birthmarks. I didn't know if I would ever get past any of that with you, but after what I witnessed today, I realize that life is short and can change in the twinkling of an eye. Once we lose someone, we can't get them back."

Elizabeth jumped up from her seat and rushed to Andrew's side. She sat next to him and squeezed his hand as she spoke to him. "Sweetie, what's happened?"

"Life. But not just to me. I'm seeing someone."

Elizabeth smiled at the knowledge of him being in a relationship.

"You all will meet her soon enough. She's great. In the midst of getting to know her, I became familiar with her sister too, and well, she passed from cancer today."

"Oh, sweetie, I'm sorry to hear that. Please give our condolences to your girlfriend and her family."

"Thanks. I will. Just being in the room with the family today, trying to comfort Renee, that's my girlfriend's name." Andrew smiled. "Watching her sister, Kim, take her last breaths and the devastation it brought to the family, made me realize that tomorrow is not promised." He looked up at Charles. "Dad, I'm still mad at you and I'm still trying to make sense of the you that raised me versus the you that raped Marie and lied to me all of these years." He stood and walked towards Charles. "But I wouldn't know what to do with myself if I lost you."

Charles released a loud sigh and his eyes watered.

"God knows I'm still hurt by you and mad at you, but I still love you." He threw his arms around him.

Charles shoulders heaved up and down as he cried and he could barely be heard through his short, choppy breaths, "I love you, too, son and I'm so glad you have forgiven me. I'm so sorry." He wrapped his arms around Andrew.

Elizabeth was overwhelmed with her tears and sobs as she held herself tightly.

Andrew finally pulled back from Charles to look him in the eyes. "I love you, Dad, but getting past the deception will be a process for me. I just know we had to start somewhere. I love you both." He looked at Elizabeth before going over to the couch and gathering her up into his arms.

Charles came behind him and squeezed his shoulder as he rubbed his wife's back.

"I know it won't be easy, son, but I'll do what it takes to gain your trust back and get my family back to the way it's supposed to be," Charles said as he covered his son and wife with the span of his arms and rested his head on theirs.

"Yes," Elizabeth cleared her throat, "we'll get back strong as a family. We love each other too much not too."

23

It had been a week since Kim had passed and Darius hadn't been to work nor had any intentions of performing at the comedy club anytime soon, if ever again. Nothing was humorous to him anymore.

Today was the day, the day of her funeral. He sat in the dark in worn gray sweats and a wrinkled T-shirt. Even though it was bright outside, his curtains were drawn, making it seem as if it were midnight in the house.

His phone rang. He wanted to ignore it as he had ignored the many other calls from his friends. He'd heard the messages from each of them. His guys had called to see how he was holding up since they knew just how much he cared for Kim, but it wasn't any of their ringtones blaring.

Maybe it was someone calling him that had no knowledge of Kim's death, his love for her, or the sheer torture his emotions and heart had been through since he saw her take her last breath. Maybe the person on the other end of the phone could provide some temporary relief from his reality that

Kim was gone. That little bit of hope propelled him to roll over on the couch and reach for his cell phone nearby on the floor, but when he answered the phone, he knew his reality would be confirmed by the other person on the phone.

"Darius?"

"Yes, Renee?"

"I just wanted to make sure that you got my messages."

"Yeah, I did." It was amazing to him how he managed to understand a word she said amidst her uneven breathing caused by her sobs. Her voice sounded so raw, grated. He could tell that she had been crying, she still was. She had called him days earlier crying and barely intelligible as she relayed to him the funeral arrangements via the voicemail she left.

"So you're coming, right?" There was a hint of hope in her voice. Darius hated that his response might further crush Renee, but he was more concerned about avoiding them all, ignoring what had become his reality just barely a week ago.

He paused before saying, "No, Renee. I'm not."

"Darius." The elevated pitch in Renee's voice let him know she was alarmed. "I know that Kim never staked claim to you or bragged that you all were in a relationship, but Darius, trust me, my sister really did care about you."

Darius literally felt a rip in his heart.

"We've never met a guy she's dated over the years. For her to smile at you when she didn't think we saw her doing it, for her to not berate you around us like we know," Renee sniffled realizing she needed to correct herself, "knew she could said a lot. She may not have shown you that she cared for you the way you're used to, but she did, Darius. I just know she did." Renee paused again, trying to calm her cries. "She even whispered to me one day that she was sad that she would never get to marry you, the man who she loved and knew loved her. That y'all would never have kids together. Darius, she loved you."

If Renee were any other person, he would have long since hung up on her, but she was too nice of a person to do that too. Her last efforted confession to cajole him into going to the funeral was too much for him. The possibility of what she said being true infuriated him all the more that Kim gave up so easily on them, that she would never be his wife, bare his children. "Renee, I gotta go. Okay?"

"Okay."

He could hear her sobs grow louder as he hung up the phone. He definitely wasn't going to the funeral now. He couldn't take seeing anyone mourn over the woman that should be alive and by his side at that very moment.

He fell back on the couch and closed his eyes for what seemed like hours to him, but in reality, only twenty minutes of visions of Kim's bright eyes and radiant smile flashed across his mind before he was interrupted by pounding at the door.

It came to him as no surprise that someone would actually show up to his house to possibly convince him to go to the funeral. It was set to start in about two hours and his guys had been calling him nonstop the night before and all of that morning, but he never answered. The same way he didn't answer his phone, he had no intention of answering his door, but the rattling of keys and hearing the lock chamber shift reminded him that at least one of the gents had a key to his place in case of an emergency.

He jumped up from his couch and dashed to the door hoping to relock it and the deadbolt before they could get in, but it was too late.

His tall and solid frame was no match for the similar physiques of the three men pressing against the other side of the door.

"Would y'all just leave already?" Darius said as he pressed against the door even though he knew he was losing the battle with keeping them out.

Vance broke through first. "I don't know why you were just wasting your time thinking you could keep all three of us out," he said as he walked through smoothing out his suit jacket and readjusting his tie.

Darius finally stood up straight as Marcus and Anthony walked past him and made themselves at home in his living room as Vance was already doing.

Darius finally closed the door, huffing and annoyed that they were there interrupting his solitude.

Marcus walked over to the curtains and opened them wide flooding the room with light.

Darius' forearm flew up to his face to shield his eyes from the bright lights he hadn't been accustomed to in about a week.

Marcus noted Darius movements and said, "I don't care. You need some light in here."

Darius ignored Marcus and rushed to the curtains to close them.

Marcus didn't contest Darius because he nodded at Vance to hit the lights and he obliged.

Darius knew there would be no winning the light battle with the brothers so he stomped over to his empty oversized arm chair and flopped down in it and shielded his face with his forearm again.

"You alright, bro?" Anthony asked.

Darius didn't respond.

Vance cocked his head looking at Anthony as if to say, 'What do you think?'. Anthony shrugged his shoulders and Vance finally took a seat on the couch across from where Darius sat. "Look, D, we can only imagine how it feels to lose the woman you just realized you love, but today's your last day to pay your respects to her. Renee called Pam even more hysterical than she's been this past week and said that she had just talked to you and you said you weren't going to the funeral. Man, don't be like that. You need to get up and get ready to go to the funeral, and judging from the scruff on your face and on your head," he looked down at his watch, "you'll need every minute of the next hour and forty minutes to get cleaned up and make it to the church on time."

Darius continued to sit in silence.

"Come on, man. I know you're hurting, but I believe you'll feel even worse if you let this day go by and not attend the funeral," Marcus said as he hit Darius on his foot dangling off the arm of the chair.

"Yeah, dude. You didn't come to the shop yesterday like I told you to get your haircut. I'll line you up real quick. Trim your beard for you, too. Your clippers are in your bathroom, right?" Anthony headed towards Darius bathroom but his steps were halted by Darius' booming voice.

"I am not going. So y'all can just leave out the same way you came." Darius jumped up from his seat and rushed to his bedroom slamming the door behind him.

"What should we do?" Anthony was the first to speak up. "Go in there and drag him out with us?"

Vance rubbed his face in and let out a loud sigh. "Naw, man. Think about how I was before I saw the light again. There was nothing y'all could say to convince me that God still cared for me after my father was senselessly killed. It took y'all praying for me and an actual encounter with Him before I came back to my senses and realized that I did need Him in my life. We just have to pray that he makes the right decision before it's too late."

"Yeah, that's all we can do is pray but we need to get to the church. With the service being all the way on the other side of town, we'll barely make it there on time," Marcus said as he looked down at his watch and headed to the door. The other gents soon followed behind him and out the door.

24

Vance, Marcus, and Anthony made it to the church in just enough time for Vance to walk in with the family next to Pam. Mr. and Mrs. Williams knew how close the ladies all were and needed all of the help she could get with trying to console Renee since her hands were full with her withered husband.

Although a week had passed since Kim transitioned, Mrs. Williams still hadn't had time to grieve in a way that a mother deserved to grieve in the loss of her child. Every time she tried to steal a few moments away to herself and breakdown or scream like what was expected of a mother who would soon have to bury their child, she would hear the loud sobs of her husband and rush to his side to prevent the onslaught of him having an asthma attack.

And when she wasn't tending to her husband, which seemed like always to her, or answering sympathy calls from loved ones and her church family, she was helping Andrew comfort Renee, who had been camped out at her house since they left the hospital after Kim passed. She returned Vance's hug before he saddled up next to Pam and allowed her tears to soak his suit jacket.

Renee looked up at Vance with sad, inquisitive eyes and he knew exactly what she was hinting at. He whispered to her, "He wouldn't come."

Renee cupped her mouth to quell her recent bout of cries brewing in her. It further saddened her that Darius wouldn't be there to pay his last respects to her sister.

Marcus went to join his wife who was already seated and Anthony followed behind him.

The music started and Mrs. Williams looked back at them letting them know it was time for them all to walk down the middle aisle of the spacious church for the funeral procession.

The church was packed with family members, friends, and even Kim's current class of students, who were busy holding each other's hands crying and consoling one another. Many of her former students were there as well.

There was a mass of hands reaching out to pat Mr. and Mrs. Williams, Renee, and Keith's hands as they took the dreaded walk up to the first pew of the church.

They opted not to have a wake before the service. They agreed that having to sit through an hour of condolences with Kim's casket open would be too much for their grieving hearts to endure.

The pastor of the church, Pastor Johnson, stood behind the podium once the family was seated. "Good morning everyone. I'm sure the family appreciates you all being here to celebrate the homegoing service of our beloved sister, Kimberly Denise Williams." He smiled all the while shaking his head. "I baptized this young woman here." He pointed to the casket. "Watched her sassy self grow up in this very church."

People spread out across the sanctuary chuckled.

"Yes, many of you all can attest to her being sassy, but we all loved her." He looked down at the paper in his hands. "The program goes as follows…"

In true Baptist style, a minister read a scripture from the Old Testament, another followed him and read a scripture from the New Testament, and yet another followed that one with a heartfelt prayer.

Pastor Johnson returned to the podium after the prayer. "And now we'll have a musical selection from one of Kim's best friends, her sister-in-law, a songbird, Monica Williams." He looked out in the audience at Monica and smiled at her before he returned to his seat.

Monica stood and took deep breaths trying to champion her feet to move, but when she looked to the left and right of her and only say Renee and Pam and realized that it was Kim laying in the closed casket in front of her, her knees buckled. She clutched her stomach and fell back down on the pew sobbing. Keith wiped his face of tears and rubbed her back as he managed to shake his head at Pastor Johnson.

Pastor Johnson understood Keith's head gesture and rose to his feet and to the mic. "That's okay. I know how close they were." He looked back over his shoulder and nodded to his wife. She rose from her chair near the pulpit and made her way to the mic stand near the organist. "My wife knew Kim, so I'm confident you all will be blessed by her choice of song."

First Lady Johnson brought the congregation to their feet and hands in the air as she belted out "Encourage Yourself in The Lord" by the gospel singer Donald Lawrence.

Mrs. Williams could feel the levy guarding her tears readying itself to break but her husband's erratic breathing and heaving chest forced her to still her emotions. She was grateful for Andrew's presence as he worked to calm her living daughter bearing the sight of her deceased daughter. And she knew that Keith was hurting as he had always been the protector of his sisters, but she knew his desire to keep his pregnant wife calm made him like her, putting their emotions aside to tend to their loved ones. She laughed to herself thinking that's what Kim had been doing over the years, hiding her cancer from everyone. She realized that her kids had all gotten that trait from her.

Mrs. Williams was brought from her epiphany by Pastor Johnson's voice.

She continued rubbing her husband's back as she adjusted in her seat and put her attention back on the speaker.

"In knowing that Kim was a straight to the point person, the family has eliminated many parts of a funeral you may be used to, so there won't be another song, but next we'll have two-minute remarks from family and friends and then I'll return to give the eulogy."

Renee sat balled up as one person after the other shared vivid memories of Kim.

Mrs. Williams looked back for a second to see that there was no one else in line to give remarks. She sighed and stood figuring she would be the last one to speak about her ball of fire of a daughter before Pastor Johnson gave the eulogy, but a small commotion behind her stifled her attempt to move forward. She looked near the back of the church to see that Darius had showed up and was working to get to the empty seat in the middle of the pew, just past Marcus and his wife.

She smiled at motioned for him to come forward.

He shook his head from side to side.

She dismissed his rejection and continued to smile. "Come here." She mouthed.

Darius was stumped. How could he say no after that? To the mother of the woman he loved? He took a deep breath and walked back past Marcus, his wife, and Anthony seated at the end of the pew. He made his way up to Mrs. Williams and leaned in to hear her speak to him.

"I would appreciate if you went up there and said something about her. I think you saw a side of her that many of us hadn't seen."

He would honor her request. Readying himself to walk to the podium designated for guests to speak, he gripped the endcap of the pew and bit his lip before he pulled away and walked to the podium.

The gents immediately stood and lined the wall nearest to him not knowing how he would react given his outburst the night she passed.

Mrs. Williams sat in her seat overwhelmed with her emotions, imagining that if Darius and Kim were as close as she suspected they were that him going up there would be hard for him, but the day was hard on everybody. She saw the love they had for one another at the hospital and knew that it might be beneficial for him if he had closure by speaking up about her in front of everyone.

She'd never heard Kim talk about a significant other, although she wished it were the case for her oldest daughter. She knew that all of them had gotten closer to one another over the past few years as a result of Pam being with Vance. She'd been told about Darius from Renee. If there were any man she wanted Kim to end up with, it would've been Darius. She didn't know much about him, but if his commitment to being there during her last days was any indication of what kind of man he was, then he was the one for her Kimberly.

She widened her smile at him as best as she could as she watched him grip the podium with everything in him.

He stood there unsure of where to focus his gaze as he focused on what he would say, but one thing he knew for sure was that he couldn't look at the casket to the right of him.

Realizing that he had been up there for a while under the scrutiny of many faces who didn't even know who he was versus the sad stares of his friends and the sisterhood, he thought it was best to speak up. He cleared his throat from the week's worth of emotions clogged in it and opened his mouth, but when he said hello, he didn't even recognize his own voice. He cleared his throat again. "Hello." He looked into the crowd. He would rather focus on those he didn't know rather than look into the pitying gazes of those who knew his relationship to Kim. "I apologize for being late. In all honesty, and the way K…" He stopped unable to bring himself to say her name knowing she wouldn't talk back to him. He took a deep breath and willed himself to continue on. "Keeping it honest the way she would, I wasn't going to come at first. As a comedian, I pride myself on being able to make others laugh yet at the moment, no jokes come to mind." He lowered his head in a brief attempt to keep the tears stinging his eyes not to fall.

He mindlessly looked over at the casket. It wasn't just the closed casket that he knew contained her body that unnerved him, but it was the large poster of her near the head of her casket. Her life-sized smile stumped him and really caused his tears to flow. He kept his head down taking more time to compose himself. Choking again on his emotions, he said, "I just don't understand how a vivacious woman such as Kim, so full of life, always one to cut someone with her tongue if need be can no longer talk anymore. Can no longer be herself. Be with me."

He looked head on to the casket and spoke to Kim. "You were supposed to be my wife. We were supposed to grow old together, have a funny son like me and a feisty daughter like you. Why'd you leave me?" He gripped the sides of the podium as he buckled from the weight of his grief. Sniffles from many in the church filled the air. The gents rushed up to usher his heaving body to his seat.

25

After Mrs. Williams saw to it that Darius's friends had him under control, she took her time getting to the podium. She stood there looking regal in her purple suit and hat. Like the greatly respected woman that she was, she had always given off an air of authority and power and that day was no different. It seemed as if everyone, even infants who had been fussy during the service, seemed to hush and focus their undivided attention on her. She smiled at them all recalling various memories of how most of them had interacted with Kim over the years.

She took a deep breath and shook her head some before she cleared the tremble in her throat. "No mother should outlive their child, but you know what?" Her eyebrows raised. "I'm blessed to have experienced my daughter, Kimberly Denise Williams, for the thirty-four years I did."

She looked over at Renee on the first pew buckled over sobbing. "My sweet babies," she said more to herself than to anyone else. "We were at the house the day after Kim passed and my other daughter, her triplet, Renee, said she prayed for God to heal Kim, but He didn't. But brothers and sisters," she looked out smiling at the audience, "He did. Just not the way any of us may have wanted Him to. You know, we can be selfish sometimes wanting to keep our loved ones with us know matter how old they may be or how sick they may have gotten. We're so used to living in this world that we clearly forget the one beyond this one that God promised us is greater. I believe that if we really sat back and thought about just how glorious heaven really is, we would all jump up with outstretched hands and ask God to receive us right now, at this very moment."

"My Lord," one of the mothers in the church shouted.

"Kim is healed, we just didn't see it's manifestation here on earth, but if you believe in the God that I know, then you know that He promised there wouldn't be any pain in heaven. My daughter is healed."

"Yes God." A younger woman who Kim once sang in the youth choir with jumped up shouting.

Mrs. Williams gave a fierce side-eye as she continued on. "Now I know that some of you all know that Kim wasn't the holiest person you'd ever met." Loud bursts of laughter erupted over the congregation. "But I did raise her to be a God-fearing woman. Most importantly, before she transitioned, she recommitted her life to Christ so I believe that she is healed in heaven. We're here to celebrate her homegoing, since heaven is her new home. But how many of you all know that a funeral is more so for the living than for the dead?"

"You better tell them," one of the ministers called out from the pulpit.

"I see so many of you all here crying, probably remembering the good times you had with Kim and trust me, I want to join in crying with you all. After all, she was my daughter. I carried her along with her brother and sister for close to eight months. I felt her kicks and connected with her before anyone of you all did. Now I didn't say that to sound self-righteous or anything, but I said that to say that my cries should be heard louder than anyone else up in here since this is the point of the service where people should be sharing fond memories of Kim and how much we all loved her, but I would rather take the time to talk to you all. If God came back at this very moment, are you anchored in the Lord? Have you given Him your all?

"Kim was so defeated days before she passed and not because of the cancer running rampant in her body, but because she felt she hadn't fully lived out her purpose on earth. So my earnest question for you today is, are you? Are you living your best life? Believe it or not, she loved teaching. It always fulfilled her in a way she said no other profession could. It took us some doing before her time expired on earth to get her not to beat herself for living more so for God than she did. So again, I'll ask you, what are you doing with your time on earth? I would hate for anyone else to bear the agony of having a conversation with a near death loved one questioning how they spent their time on earth." She looked over at Renee who had managed to sit up and was resting her head on Andrew's shoulder.

"Hopefully I have some of you all sitting there thinking about the answer to my question, but you don't have to come up with a long drawn out plan right now to live better on earth. You can start by smiling at your neighbor. Holding a door open for an elderly person. Helping a child do their homework. Stop being so busy through the day that you don't even take time to listen to the wind rustling past you or look at the pretty colors of the flowers. Just slow down from the busyness that life, day to day, can bring. Cherish life more by being kinder to others. Change your eating habits if you need to. Let go of some bad habits. Start that company that you've always wanted to. Take that dance class you've been nervous to do. If it's something that's healthy for you and you've been desiring it for a long time, get to it. Don't let the curtain almost close on the last scene of your life and you're left with regrets of what you could've, should've done. But most importantly, if you haven't, now is the best time if any to accept God as your Lord and personal savior. It doesn't matter that this is a funeral. God wants your undivided attention, your heart, and He'll take it anywhere you give it to Him." She looked back to the pulpit at the pastor and he nodded his head giving her the go-ahead to continue with the altar call.

She turned back to the congregation and stretched her hands forward as the organist began to play. A few members of the choir stood behind mics and began to softly sing, "We offer Christ to you, oh my brother, we offer Christ to you, oh my sister, He will give you brand new life, life abundantly, so come, come on, to Christ…"

She rejoiced as many filled the aisle and made their way to the front of the church stopping short of the casket. Intercessors from the church met them there and began to pray for each of them.

Mrs. Williams smiled as she took her seat and her husband wrapped his arms around her. He realized that she hadn't even cried yet because she had been so busy looking after him. The longer and tighter he held her the more she relaxed into his arms and allowed her tears to flow freely until her sobs rang out into the tall ceilings of the church.

Renee straightened herself up and began to rub her mother's arm trying to be a comfort to her.

Monica released Keith and he went and knelt in front of his mother and squeezed her hands as she continued to weep openly.

Pastor Johnson stood and walked back to the podium in the pulpit. "Well ladies and gentleman, sisters and brothers, there's no need for me to give a eulogy, Sister Williams pretty much said everything I was gonna say."

Many in the congregation smiled or laughed as they wiped away the last of their tears. Those who were at the altar and had given their lives to Christ, returned to their seats.

Pastor Johnson nodded to the funeral directors and they began to prepare the body for the final viewing.

26

Everyone sat around the family table in the dining hall of the church at the repast. They had not too long ago returned from the burial site. In the limo ride there, Monica, Pam, and Renee held each other tightly and cried together with the realization that they were going to bury their best friend and sister.

Once there, Renee and Keith had to take turns upholding their mother and father as they lowered Kim's casket into the ground, and then Andrew and Monica had to comfort Renee and Keith as best as they could.

Those who stayed for the repast had fell into the comfortable state of talking and laughing with one another with memories of Kim. Occasionally, someone would come past the family table and extend their condolences to the Williams' with a handshake, hug, or a kiss.

In the midst of one of the mothers of the church talking with Mrs. Williams, Marcus made his way up to the table and bent over to whisper something to Renee. Her facial expressions ran the gamut of emotions from glee to sorrow as Marcus spoke to her.

"Excuse me." Renee jumped up abruptly from her seat and ran to the bathroom. Andrew was almost on her heels when Monica patted him on his arm. "We'll go and see about her." Monica and Pam walked arm in arm to the bathroom.

Darius excused himself from the table and out of their sight. Marcus didn't even bother to rejoin his wife at the table they were sitting in, but rather trailed behind Vance and Anthony to search for Darius.

***

They found Darius sitting at the front of the church staring at the supersized picture of Kim with her brilliant smile.

They approached him cautiously.

He briefly looked back over his shoulder and saw his friend's trepidation. He turned back to face her picture and braced his elbows on his knees before he said, "Y'all ain't gotta tip toe around me." He wrung his hands together.

"We ain't scared of you or nothing. We just didn't wanna scare you with any sudden movements." Vance shrugged his shoulders trying to ward off the unbelieving stares of Marcus and Anthony spiraling his way.

"So, how are you really holding up?" Marcus asked as he walked past Darius and sat near him on the pew.

"Holding up? More like I'm barely holding on. I just don't believe it. I don't believe that she's gone. I mean, I get I didn't know right away that she was the one for me like y'all did with your wives, but when it hit me, I mean really hit me, I was ready to give her my all, but she just up and left me." Darius dropped his head in his big hands.

"I can only imagine how you must feel, but D, can't you say that you're a better man because of the time you spent with her?" Vance said as he sat in the empty space to the right of Darius.

"But I would be an even better man if she were still here, with me." He kept his head low.

"You don't have to get over her today, tomorrow, you may never get over her. I believe you'll always carry her spirit and what you two shared with you, but I do know that you'll move on in time. Use her as an inspiration to move forward and not a stronghold that will hinder you from moving forward. You know Vance and I know how either of those scenarios can work out," Marcus said.

"Hey, all that matters in my case is that Dad's death is no longer a stronghold for me," Vance said to his brother.

"You're right, Marcus. I know I'll never get over her, I don't think I want to, but I will use all of this for my good," Darius said.

"What do you mean?" Anthony asked as he came closer to the men.

"You all know that she refused to talk to me all of that time I was with her at the hospital, but Renee told me that one day when they talked when she put me out of the room, that Kim wanted me to make sure that I lived my best life while I could. You know, live out my purpose."

The other guys nodded their heads in understanding.

"Don't get me wrong, I love being a financial adviser, but y'all know how much I love comedy, making people laugh. It's my real passion. Phil down at the club has been acting like my agent for a while, sending tapes of my set out to people. Well he found out a few weeks before I found out that Kim was sick how a manager for a tour with some big hitters in the comedy arena wants me to be an opening act for their world tour starting next month."

That's great, man." Vance slapped Darius on his shoulder.

"Thanks bro. Well, I'm gonna see where it leads. I have a lot of vacation time saved up, so I'll take some time off from work and see what being a comedian really has in store for me."

"Greatness. Greatness," Anthony said.

Darius stood causing Marcus and Vance to follow suit. "Give me a minute guys. I'll catch up with you all back in the dining hall."

The fellas shook up with him before heading back to the repast.

Darius turned and stuffed his hands in his pockets as he stared at Kim's picture mounted on the easel. "You never let me tell you how I really felt about you all of that time I was at the hospital with you, but now you can't shut me up." He smiled just imagining the sassy response she would give him.

He let out a long sigh and rubbed his head with both hands before continuing on. "You can't shut me up now, so here goes. I love you, Kim. I'm so mad at you that you left me, but I'm happy that you aren't suffering anymore. I don't know if this is a bad thing to say, but if you were still here, I wouldn't even think about going on this tour. I guess from all the jokes I told, you knew I loved comedy. Why couldn't we share our passions more with one another while you were alive? Man, I wish you could answer me right now." He sniffled. "I hate that Renee had to tell me that you loved me rather than your stubborn self doing it. But that's okay, I knew you did."

He paused pretending like she questioned how he knew. "I just did. For as much as you loved to talk, your actions spoke loud, too." He walked closer to her picture and lowered his voice as if he only wanted her to hear him. "Maybe I shouldn't bring this up here, but I remember one time you called me over to your place and all I could do was shake my head and laugh at you. You had on one of those sexy lingerie outfits I couldn't wait to take off you. Color Me Badd's hit song "I Wanna Sex You Up" was playing through your speakers as you stood in the doorway and invited me in. You looked amazing to me that night like you always did, but to be honest, that night I knew I wanted more than just sex with you. You know as well as I know that I definitely loved our time together in bed. You were open to letting me treasure your body, but baby, I wanted so much more than that early on. I just stayed cool about it because I could see how you were and I didn't wanna push you away, not to mention I was still scared of my feelings at the time. You were the one that controlled everything between us in the bedroom, on the couch, the countertop, pretty much any space that was available." He licked his lips slowly remembering their times together. "I could tell from the way you screamed at the end of each time we were together that you were satisfied. You always exhaled one last time as that lazy, but extremely sexy smile crept on your face and a glint of vulnerability shined in your eyes. But you would compose yourself quickly and put me out. I never wanted to before you, but after we finished, I wanted to cuddle with you, just talk to you until the wee hours of the morning. Why'd Renee have to be the one to tell me that you loved me?" He reached out and lightly traced her lips on the picture with the pad of his pointer finger. "I knew it, but I just wish I could've heard you say those words to me.

"You were so stubborn in the hospital that you wouldn't say it to me or let me say it to you. But we can't turn back the hands of time. I'll just work on letting you go day by day. Thanks for giving me the push with my passion. I love you, Kim, and I'm certain I always will." He pressed two of his fingers to his lips before he pressed those same two fingers against her lips on her picture. He wiped the lone tear from his face and shoved his hands in the pockets of his fitted slacks before he pivoted and walked back towards the dining hall.

***

Pam and Monica finally found the bathroom Renee was in and locked the door behind them when they saw that no one else was in there other than Renee. She was held up in a stall crying loudly.

"Renee, sweetie, you can come out. It's just us in here," Pam said choked up. She hated seeing Renee hurt so much over losing Kim.

"We're here for you, Renee. Come out and be with us," Monica said as she sat down on the seat near the door.

Renee finally opened the door and came out wiping her runny nose with tissue. With puffy and red eyes, she looked up at them crying and broken and realized that she had been so consumed with her grief that she hadn't taken time over the past week to see just how they were coping with losing Kim.

She rushed over to Monica first and bent over and gave her a long, warm hug before turning her attention to Pam and embracing her with as much love as she'd shown Monica. "I'm sorry you two. I've been so consumed with dealing with losing my sissy that I didn't even bother to be there for you all. I know you all loved her just as much as I did."

"If that's possible," Monica said as she stood and grabbed tissue from the countertop to wipe her nose.

"I know it is," Renee replied. "Kim and I were sisters by blood, but the four us, we're sisters by love. We had an unbreakable bond." She yelped at the mention of referring to their bond in past tense.

"We still do." Pam admonished her as she grabbed and squeezed Renee's hand. "I admit that it's still unbelievable that she's not here, not in here with us right now snapping on us for being all sentimental, but I just know that we'll get through this together, in time."

"Yeah, we'll never forget her and it's all the times that we shared together that will keep us together and her alive in our memories," Monica said as she hugged Renee.

"I know, it's just still so unbelievable and hurts so bad. If she would've stuck around she could've met him." Renee walked away from them and braced herself on the countertop as she let her tears flow freely.

"Who, sweetie?" Pam walked closer to Renee and rubbed her back.

"My son." Renee sprang upright with bright eyes. "That's what sent me rushing in here. Marcus just got back word from a friend of his in D.C. that went and spoke with my son's adoptive family. He convinced them to let me see him. I'm really gonna meet him." Her hands shook as she looked at them.

Pam and Monica smiled and hugged each other, but their joy was halted as Renee's smile faltered and she continued talking. "If only I'd been able to pull myself together before she passed, I could've went there and convinced them to let me be in his life. I could've brought him here for a visit or at least went there with her to visit him." Renee buried her face in her hands as she sobbed.

"Oh, sweetie. You can't beat yourself up over that." Again, Pam drew closer to Renee and pulled her in for a hug.

"Maybe in Kim's twisted way of getting things done, her sickness and death gave you the push you needed to reach out to him, especially since you want to be in his life so much," Monica said as she stood next to Renee and rubbed her arm.

Renee found herself smiling as Monica's half-witted revelation registered to her. "As crazy as it may be, you're right. If the threat of Kim dying hadn't come to us so suddenly, I would've continued putting off my desire to do something about connecting with Isaiah. His name is Isaiah." Her smile stretched wide across her face. "Seeing Kim the way she was hit me how life could change so suddenly. I didn't wanna live anymore with the regret of him not being in my life."

Pam and Monica wiped the happy tears from their eyes as they saw how Renee glowed saying her son's name.

"I just wish she would've found another way other than leaving me to get me to connect with him."

"We do, too. So, how soon will you see him?" Pam asked in anticipation.

"I'm getting on the plane first thing next Friday morning headed to D.C."

"You need one us to go with you?" Monica asked as she squeezed both Pam and Renee's hands.

"No, this is something I need to do on my own."

"But you don't have to. We're here for you." Pam's voice was stern. "We each have dealt with things over the past couple of years that we were either too embarrassed or bull headed to tell the others about. Looking back, we wouldn't have carried each of our burdens as long as we did, nor have to bear the heavy weight of them if we would've only drawn on the strength that each of us have to offer one another. So no, you don't have to do it alone. We're going with you. We'll be right there to support you through it all," Pam said.

Renee's smile inched wider and wider. "I know now not to hold back from you all, but I'm okay with going out there by myself, in fact I need to. I know how overwhelming it can be when a child is reunited with the parent that gave them up, no matter what the circumstances were. So I'm going to meet with his parents Friday night and then they'll introduce me to him Saturday morning. We wanna ease him into getting to know me."

"We're so proud of you, Renee, but are you sure you don't want one of us or both of us to go with you?" Pam asked.

Renee smirked as she shook her head.

"What?" Monica's eyes narrowed in on Renee and her forehead crinkled.

"Nothing. Just when I told Andrew what I was going to do, he insisted that he go with me. He won't take no for an answer." She fidgeted with her hands.

"Renee, what?" Pam asked curiously.

"Well, oddly, I want him to go. I want to share the experience with him."

"And there's nothing wrong with that." Monica laughed. "We know you haven't dated since Ted, but it's totally okay for you to be into Andrew and want to share experiences with him," Monica said.

"I know. I know that he can relate to my situation and has even helped me to see some things from a perspective that even my years as a social worker may not have prepared me for. I just have to get used to the idea of being able to trust him."

"We all can see that you can trust Andrew. He's a good guy," Pam said.

Renee's smile would've probably measured at a thousand watts if it were humanly possible. "I know I can and my sissy helped me to see that before she passed. She told me not to hold back with Andrew. She told me to love him with all of my heart, which I do," she giggled, "and that God would work everything else out in our lives. And He's doing just that. Andrew is back on speaking terms with his mom and dad and is trying to repair their relationship and I get to meet my son soon."

"That's so good to hear about Andrew," Monica said.

"Yup. That was one of things that made me still not sure about us even though I know we really care about one another, but now that that's being rebuilt, he and I can move forward. I believe successfully. Besides, you and Vance are married and you and Keith are about to have your third baby, I can't depend on you all the way I did in the past when all of us were single."

"That is so not true," Monica said. She and Pam found themselves wrapping their arms tightly around Renee. "Remember, just like Whitney Houston's song says, you can count on me through thick and thin a friendship that will never end when you are weak I will be strong, helping you to carry on. Call on me, I will be there. Don't be afraid. Please believe me when I say, count on me." The trio found themselves singing the lyrics to the song in sync as they walked out of the bathroom together.

Other Books Available

<u>Sisterhood Chronicles Series</u>
Underneath It All
Discovery
Untold
When It Happens To You
All Things Considered

<u>Forever Friends Series</u>
Catch Me If You Can
It's Complicated

<u>Limelight Series</u>
Hues
Tones
Vision

<u>Standalone Titles</u>
After All Is Said & Done
The Bid Catcher: Distinguished Gentlemen Series

*(Best if you read Forever Friends series before
reading Sisterhood Chronicles 3)*

COMING SOON

The Kissing Game: Love Alive 1

ABOUT THE AUTHOR

Anita Davis is a former elementary teacher born and raised in Chicago. Although she wrote short stories much of her childhood, she didn't unlock and cultivate her passion as a writer until she became a writing teacher for middle school students. The more she had to create sample writings for her students, the more she realized her passion and ability to tell stories in the written form. She decided to hone her craft as a writer by completing her Master of Fine Arts in Creative Writing via National University. She now pursues writing books most of her time, in addition to being a flight attendant. Anita seeks to encourage, engage, and entertain her readers.

She is Co-Founder of Book Euphoria, a group of Chicago authors bound by their love of literature. Book Euphoria hosts literary events and they also founded the empowerment movement, Black Girl Passion.

Anita writes contemporary romantic women's fiction and seeks to encourage, engage, and entertain her readers.

authoranitadavis@gmail.com
www.authoranitadavis.com
Facebook: Anita Davis and Author page: Author Anita Davis
Instagram: @authoranitadavis   Twitter: @_AnitaDavis